GREED

LOVE IS CURE, VOL. 1 - VICES & VIRTUES SERIES

BOOK THREE

BROOKELYN MOSLEY

85 MEDIA LLC

More By Brookelyn Mosley

Links to the below stories can be found here (https://brookelynmosley.com/ebooks-paperbacks/)

Novels/Novellas/Novelettes/Series

- No Fraternizing, Pt. 1
- No Fraternizing, Pt. 2
- No Fraternizing, Pt. 3
- First Came Love: The Love, Hate & Revenge Prequel
- Love, Hate & Revenge, Pt. 1
- Love, Hate & Revenge, Pt. 2
- Love, Hate & Revenge, Pt. 3
- Girl Code
- Mr. & Mrs. Jones
- Forbidden: An Anthology
- They Call Me Mello
- A Love Deferred
- Indecent Arrangement
- Last Comes Love
- Ebb & Flow
- PRIDE
- Meant To Be
- LUST
- Loveless
- GREED
- Rekindled
- My First, My Last

• ENVY

• Ready or Not

• So This is Love

• Home Before Midnight

• GLUTTONY

• When Luke Met Juliette

• When Life Gives You Sunsets

• In Love, I Trust

• Wrath

• Sloth

Short Stories

• Unsilent Knight

• Twice In Love

• Home For Christmas

ByBK Exclusives

Bed Bully
Stuck
LHR Rewind Series
Home Before Midnight
Maybe This Time Will Be Different
Lovekilla
Incoming Call
Rough
WYD
Drinks on Me
Cali & Lee
Ray & Jay
Living Out a Love Song
Glimpses
One Mic
With Love, Ayanna & Dallas
Just Friends
Lena's Ex-File
Dream Boss
Chateau Luxure

Click Here to see if new exclusive shorts have been added to ByBK
(Copy + paste this link if the above link doesn't work: https://
bybrookelynmosley.com/collections/ebooks)

Acknowledgments

A loving thank you to my amazing husband who is without a doubt one of my biggest supporters. Your support is worth its weight in gold. A special thank you to my reading family. To the active members in my Facebook reading group, my beloved beta readers for this project, and my supporters across all social medias. You all have embraced my brand of writing and I'm beyond appreciative of it. Shout out to the readers who have reached out to me to share your thoughts regarding my books. I thank you for keeping me motivated and excited to create new projects for you. When I write, I keep you in mind. Thank you for your support. It's my soul food.

Message from the Author

Thank you for purchasing your copy of *GREED*. *GREED* is the third book in the *Love Is Cure, Vol. 1 – Vices & Virtues* series and runs somewhat parallel to my bittersweet love story, *Last Comes Love* (*LCL*). What this means is that some scenes that appear in *LCL* appear in *GREED*, just from a different perspective. You don't have to read *LCL* first to read *GREED* but you will experience a bit of a spoiler if you haven't read LCL yet. However, if you've never read a bittersweet love story, reading *LCL* after might make things a bit easier to digest. Although *GREED* is book three in the *Love Is Cure, Vol. 1 – Vices & Virtues* series, it does not have to be read in any particular order. All of the books in this series are standalone and can be read out of order. So if *GREED* is your first read in the series, you are more than welcomed to start there! Again, thank you for your support. Please consider leaving a review once you have completed *GREED*. I look forward to your feedback. Thank you and enjoy the ride.

Love,
Brookelyn.

Dedicated to the saints and the sinners...

ONE

"Grandmother, how are you this morning?"

I leaned back in my leather office chair, fingers stroking the smooth hairs of my beard. I'd been practicing this phone call in the mirror for a week.

"Great, Bryant. I'm great," she chirped. "Thanks so much for asking. I'm so happy you called too."

I smiled.

"It's so good to hear your voice, grandson. I hardly hear it as often."

"Yeah..." My eyes shifted over to my office windows. "It's been an awfully busy few months for me."

I wasn't lying about that part. As the CEO of a multitude of companies, I barely had enough time to sleep. But I wasn't complaining in the least. This is the life I've always wanted. Built from the ground up by me. Of course I received a familial boost along the way, but all that Bryant Greene earned, Bryant Greene acquired via ambition and hard work.

"Well, that I can believe." She giggled. "How's the salt factory and flour mill holding up? I haven't visited either in ages."

"Great!" I moved my view along the edges of my custom-made L-shaped office desk. "We've just installed a few more machines to expedite the milling process at the flour mill and have signed fifteen new contracts with gourmet markets to place our salt on their shelves. We're also in talks with a bread company. They're interested in us being a flour and salt supplier for their products."

"Oh, Bryant, that is marvelous news! Your grandfather would be so proud."

I beamed, pleased with the verbal pat on the back.

"You know, when he gifted you the flour mill and salt factory, everyone thought he was insane to do so to a 17-year-old, but I trusted his vision when he noticed something in you that others hadn't yet."

"That he did."

"Now look at you; a billionaire. My grandson is a billionaire. Oh, the heavens!"

I adjusted the knot on my tie. "Well, grandmother, if you really want to brag, they're calling me a multi-billionaire now."

She laughed a hearty laugh and squealed. I couldn't help but to laugh too.

Truthfully, I didn't have the multi-billions in my literal possession but my companies, investments, and overall net worth had reached the $6.1 billion calculation and the year hadn't even ended yet.

"Anyway." She cleared her throat. "My busy grandson did not just call to shoot the breeze with this old lady, so what do *I* owe the pleasure of this phone call from *you*?"

"Grandmother, come on now." I chuckled. "Of course, I only called to speak with my grandmother. I haven't spoken to you in months."

I hoped like hell that was convincing enough. She knew her grandson well. As soothing as it was, I absolutely didn't call just to hear her voice. My dear ol' granny was sitting on my next money move - land in a prime real estate location in Upstate New York. Morgansville had become a prime real estate location overnight, and I wanted in. Buildings were going up all over that compact town. Condominiums and mixed-use developments. It was a predominantly black area, but investors had other plans. Honestly? I couldn't concern myself with the latter when there was so much money on the table up for grabs.

"Aw, Bryant, that is so sweet to think of your grandmother. You have always been my favorite you handsome devil you."

I could feel her smiling on the other end of my phone.

Perfect.

"So, uh, grandmother, tell me - how are things?"

"Fabulous," she gushed. "Simply fabulous! After your cousin's wedding, I have plans to charter a flight to Ghana with a few girl-friends."

"Nice." I nodded slowly, impressed. "Ghana is beautiful."

"Isn't it?! Oh, Bryant, you must go sometime soon. You work so hard. You deserve to treat yourself to a little getaway."

"This is true."

"But before I even leave, I must complete the renovations of the extra room I'm building in the mansion. A little girl cave I've been craving since the summer."

"Girl cave, huh?" I chuckled. "So, uh, on the subject of reno-vations..."

"*Mm-hmm...?*"

I closed one eye and asked, "How's the property in Morgansville?"

"Hmmm... Morgansville, Morgansville," she repeated to herself, something she often did when she tried recalling something she'd forgotten. "Oh, Morgansville! Wow. I've forgotten all about that old thing. It's well, I suppose."

"*Yes,*" I mouthed.

"You suppose?" I questioned. "You don't check up on it?"

"Well, no. Can't even remember the last time I've seen it. Now trust me, the property means plenty to me. It's like a family heirloom but sadly, I hardly visit."

"Hmph." I drummed a rhythm on my desk with my fingertips to count the seconds before going in for the kill. I couldn't sound too eager. "You know... *I* can manage it."

"Hmm, would you? Oh, no. It's such an old property, Bryant, nothing like the properties you're used to working with. The house and land it's built on means the world to me, but I could never burden you with something like that."

"Oh, grandmother, please. It wouldn't be a burden at all. Knowing that you love it so much, it would be my pleasure."

"You know what else is pleasurable, my loving grandson? Dating."

I snorted a laugh. "Grandmother—"

"Are you dating anybody?"

I shut my eyes and dropped my head back between my shoulders. Bit my tongue to keep from grunting on the line.

Grandmother was a matchmaker in her youth. Had an office, business cards, and actual clients. Was responsible for a few love connections, including that of my parents who were sailing the Atlantic as we spoke. They retired that spring and left New York on a two-year-long excursion they'd embarked on just that month, with no plans of returning on American soil anytime soon.

As happy as my parents were in their thirty-plus years union, I just wished grandmother didn't attempt to achieve the same for me.

"I *am* dating, actually," I lied.

"Wonderful Bryant, oooh!" she cooed, excitement laced in her tone. "Is she as great as I think she is? Is she the one?"

"Yup." I squeezed my lids shut and cringed. "And it's serious, too. Can you believe that?"

God, I hope she did.

Relationships were the last thing on my mind. The absolute last thought I had in a day. In fact, I hadn't thought of a relationship until this very moment when my grandmother made me lie to her.

"I can! I absolutely must meet her!"

"Yes, you must. One day grandmother. Some time in the future."

I'd committed my time to money, that was my focus. My commitment to my earning potential was so serious, I had the dollar sign tatted on my left ring finger to prove it.

"One day *real* soon and in the very *near* future," my grandmother insisted. "I'll be in the city on Saturday for your cousin Addison's final bridal fitting. I can meet the love of your life then."

I gulped the air. "Uh... what?"

"You'll be at Addison's New Year's Eve nuptials, right? In Long Island? Of course you will! She told me all about you giving her and her fiancé an early wedding gift by footing a generous portion of the bill. I'm so thrilled it will be at the *Gold Coast Castle*. That's where that handsome R&B singer and his wife wedded last year, too."

I slid to the edge of my seat. "Yes, grandmother, The Joneses, I know. And yes, I'll be there. Now, about you meeting my girlfriend this weekend—"

"Yes! I'm excited to see her. Oh, I'm sure she is a rare gem if she's caught your eye."

"Shit," I mumbled to myself.

"What's that Bryant?"

"I said, *she* sure is."

I was up and out of my seat, walking my way to my slanted office window to peer out of it. The building and the land it sat on belonged to me. I'd bought the land five years prior and financed the construction of the building I now stood in. Even sectioned a portion of real estate and designated it as a public space for employees and visitors to sit out in and enjoy. It was relaxing to see nothing in the distance, and what my eyes fell on belonged to me.

"Great, so Saturday it is! I'm thinking brunch or an early lunch? Oooh! I'm so excited to meet your girlfriend, Bryant, or your potential wife perhaps?"

I inhaled an encouraging breath and on my exhale said, "One step at a time, grandmother."

"I'll tell you what?" she began. "At our meet-up we can discuss the property and you managing it while I get to learn all about your new girlfriend. We can feed two birds with one seed."

I dropped my head forward and pinched the innermost corners of my eyes. "Sounds like a plan."

The moment I ended the call with my grandmother, I dropped myself down onto my leather office chair and grunted.

"What the *fuck* was that Bryant?!" I scolded. "Where the hell are you going to find a girlfriend you don't even have in time for the weekend?"

My intentions for the call was to ease into the land my grandmother had in her possession. Investors offered to pay big dividends for the acquisition of that land. I had plans to slip in there an agreement involving my private equity and venture capital firm just to ensure I had a lucrative share of their development plans because it would surely bring in bank. All I had to do was get my grandmother to agree to let me take the property off her hands, which I knew she'd do. She'd do anything for the grandson who carried the surname of her husband as his first name. But no, I just had to lie.

"Mr. Greene," I heard from my glass office door.

I swiveled my chair that way to see Emily, a petite blonde with sapphire eyes peering into me from the threshold. She wore a smile that was both seductive and cunning. I recognized the look because I'd seen it tons of times on other women before.

I returned a smile of my own to be polite. "Emily?"

"Oh good, you remember my name." She straightened her posture and poked her breasts out. I arched a brow. "I was just checking in to see if you needed anything."

My eyes moved to the solid gold digital clock on my desk. I'd only arrived at my office half-an-hour earlier. She'd checked in on me about fifteen minutes prior.

"Nope," I answered. "As I told you fifteen minutes earlier, I'm fine. But thank you, Emily."

She grinned. "Oh, you can call me Em."

I wrinkled my brows. "I think Emily will do just fine for me, thank you."

Emily was the brand new intern at my company, *The Greene Group*. The company operated out of the top floor of the 16-story building I owned. Each floor served as the headquarters for my businesses that ranged from my franchise dinner theaters and my private equity and venture capital firm to the glass fabrication and installation company I also owned. I'd recently purchased a waste removal corporation from a business associate desperate to get the failing business off his hands. After adding the company to my business portfolio in the fall, it had shown major growth as I'd expected. I had plans to acquire a few other failing businesses that also showed earning potential. There really was no such thing as having too many streams of income. That's the only way I understood how to make money grow.

"Okay," Emily conceded. She licked at her bottom lip slowly and I scoffed a laugh in response. "Well, if you need anything, Mr. Greene, and I do mean anything, please let me know."

I stared at her for a moment and she did the same. Ms. Emily was an aggressive one, the type a man like me had to be careful around.

"Uh-huh," I replied. "Thank you, Emily. That will be all."

She nodded her exit, closing my door behind herself.

I laughed to myself while shaking my head once I was alone again.

This was nothing new. Women and their unsubtle subtleness. It was the first lesson my father taught me when he noticed the sneaker cleaning business I started at 14-years old was taking off and the girls at my prep school were practically throwing themselves at me.

"Son," he advised, "it's a wonderful thing to be desired, but you must be careful where you place your attention. Some of those who admire you are looking to destroy you. Don't be too eager to drink from any cup, because it could be poison."

Women were beautiful to me, I loved them. Everything about them. But they were also trouble and distractions. Discipline was a must. I've learned that in this man's world, you're chasing two things - money or women. And when you're chasing one of them, the other is getting away. So I chose money. It's loyal and doesn't require much maintenance or reassurance of its worth.

I palmed my cordless office phone and pressed the # symbol to dial up my executive assistant, Chelsea.

Now, Chelsea was a Pitbull in a skirt. I'd be lost without her. She was also a lesbian who couldn't care less about my dick or touching it.

"Good morning, Mr. Greene."

"Good day, Chelsea. How's my calendar for the first half of the day?"

"Clear sir."

"Perfect. Then I will step out to run a few errands," I asserted. "I need to check on the new dinner theater being built Uptown and will be out of the office for the rest of the day."

"Would you like for me to call the car around?"

"Unnecessary," I replied. "I'll drive myself. I need the time to think."

She giggled. "You're the only person I know who finds driving in New York City to be ideal for thinking."

"The chaos is enlightening."

She scoffed a laugh. "Whatever you say, sir."

I smiled.

"I will transfer any important calls to your cell but those that are not time sensitive, I'll just send to your office phone's voice mail. Does this work?"

"As always, yes it does."

"Great, enjoy the rest of your day, Mr. Greene."

"I will thank you." I was just about to hang up when I remembered, "Oh, and one other thing, Chels."

"Sir?"

"Emily Warren, the intern who works on my floor in the mornings?"

"Yes, the new girl."

"Please speak with her regarding her conduct while at the office. She seems a bit too eager to *please me* if you catch my drift."

Chelsea scoffed another laugh. "I know exactly what you mean, sir. I'll have a talk with her right now."

"Appreciate it, Chelsea."

"Enjoy your drive, sir."

Chaos was exactly what I needed in that instance. Deciding how I would pull this brunch or lunch off with my grandmother this weekend would take an immense amount of thinking and, if I can be honest, scheming. I couldn't buy my way out of it... or could I?

Either way, it would take a miracle because as I took steps toward my walk-in closet to retrieve my black double-breasted wool coat, I had no idea where I would find a willing participant to not only accompany me to this meet-up with my grandmother but to convincingly pull off being in a relationship with *me*.

I needed that Morgansville property and I was going to get it by any means necessary.

"God help me," I said, as I exited through my office door.

Two

I swayed my head to the rhythm of the song playing on the radio while tapping my fingers to the beat. I had to turn the volume up on the music as a distraction to keep from losing my shit behind the wheel.

Traffic was insane. Of course it was insane, it was Times Square. Bumper to bumper traffic that had me sitting at yet another green light without moving.

I pressed down on the horn with my fist, then tossed my head back against the headrest. It really was no use. I wasn't going anywhere, no matter how hard I punched the horn.

"Man," I groaned, "I *hate* this fucking city. I'm about to be late!"

The destination programed in my GPS was routed for the beauty salon where I worked out of during the week, *Mane Chicks*. I scheduled my next appointment to arrive in the next hour. Another client I styled often had an early photo shoot in the city that morning and asked me to pull myself out of bed before the sun rose to hook her up for it.

New York City.

I would've been out of here a long time ago if it wasn't for all that I had here. My chair at *Mane Chicks*, my boyfriend, my best friend Joi, my life. Everything I knew was here on the east coast. But this traffic was for the birds.

I'd finally made it down the block to turn onto the next street I needed to be on to get to my destination when I rolled up on more traffic.

"God, help me," I said to myself.

A short chime interrupted the song on my phone. It was a text. A quick glance at my device displayed the thumbnail of a video on the screen.

I squinted my eyes that suddenly became big at the sight of what I saw in the freeze frame.

"You're Rocco's girl, right?"

I was making my way home on a Friday afternoon in August, minding my business as I trudged three bags on one arm and another two on the other. I'd just stopped by the market to pick up a few groceries for the weekend.

My intention was to spend most of Saturday and Sunday in bed, relaxing and spending some much needed time with my man, Rocco. We'd been working so much these past few weeks that we barely saw each other, so it seemed only right and like a logical plan.

I turned to the voice and saw this brown skin young woman, a couple years younger than me, maybe in her late 20s, with her hand on her hip and her cleavage in my face. She was cute, I'd give her that, but there was something in her spirit that was so ugly.

"Who's asking?" I replied.

"His soon to be girl," she stated assertively, snapping her neck with each word spoken.

I gave her a once-over and scoffed. Tossed my waist-length locs over my shoulder and kept walking. These fast asses around here were bold as hell these days. Knew who to try it with too. Didn't give a shit how they came off either. Just as long as they upset you, they were good.

"You can do all that shit all you want," she yelled behind me, "but remember my face."

I never wasted my time with them, never felt a need to. Now my girl, Joi, would have given little miss thang a piece of her mind and maybe her fists too.

Wait till I tell her what just happened, I thought to myself as I giggled the rest of the way to my apartment building.

I'd returned home and was placing the bags down on the counter when my boyfriend, Rocco, entered the kitchen.

"So it seems you have a little admirer," I reported, unpacking the groceries one at a time. "She just told me she's about to be your new girl."

He laughed, wrapping his arms around me and leaving a kiss on my neck. "She must not know I put no bitch above you, huh?"

"Apparently."

Not.

Apparently *not.* Well, to his defense, he didn't put her above me, just her mouth on his dick.

My eyes widened as I stared down at the thumbnail. Horns blared behind me. I reached my trembling hand for my phone to snatch it up and off the holder. Swiped in and into the message, tapping on the photo that was actually a video that played instantly.

"Yeah, Kali, just like that baby," he moaned off camera.

"Kali" slipped his dick in and out of her mouth, sloppily running her tongue up and down the length of him.

She released him long enough to ask, "You like that, Rocco?"

"I love it, baby, damn," he groaned.

My pressure rose when she peeked down at the lens of the phone, our eyes meeting as she grinned on the head of my boyfriend's dick, then reached her hand toward the screen.

The recording suddenly stopped.

I sat frozen for a few seconds.

The honking of the horns grew louder behind me, fueling my rage.

"Move it, lady!" I heard shouted from the car behind me.

"Come on and drive already!" yelled another driver.

But it was all a blur. I had a feeling deep in my gut that Rocco had been cheating, but I just needed the proof. And now that I had the proof, I wished I could unsee it.

I stared out of my windshield, my view slowly clouding with tears. My chest heaved up and down uncontrollably. I was breathing, clearly I was breathing, but my breaths were doing nothing to keep me calm. Ironically, the more I drew in air, the angrier I got because I realized how real the moment was. This was not a dream. It was a living nightmare.

"Wait." I glanced at the paused video on my screen. "Is that my fucking couch they're on? He got this girl in my apartment?!"

Three short breaths later... I finally snapped.

"Motherfucker!" I yelled in my seat. Before I knew it, my rage exploded out of me and materialized into me punching the steering wheel, wishing it were his face.

"Motherfucker!" I screamed again, this time stomping my foot and flailing my arms to add effect. I swear I was aiming for the floor of the driver's side, but somehow my foot landed hard and firm on the gas pedal.

Like a flash, the tires screeched loudly, and the car catapulted forward about two feet before the vehicle ahead of me stopped it dead in its tracks.

The sound of twisted metal and broken glass shattered the state I was in. I smashed right into the car in front of me and hard. So hard, my body jerked forward in my seat. My locs tousled wildly around my head.

By the time the back of my head slammed against my headrest with a hard thud, I gasped.

"Oh shit!"

Smoke seeped out the crumpled hood of my car. I slapped my hand to my mouth to cover my shock.

"Oh. *Shit*!" I repeated, this time into my hand.

The door of the car in front of me swung open.

Before the guy could step out, my leather boots were already on the asphalt. Out of my car, I fixed my eyes on the front end of my ride before rolling my view over to his bumper.

"OH SHIT!" I hollered this time. "Oh, my God, I did *not* just do that."

"What the hell?!" I heard to my left.

I turned my head to the voice, my eyes connecting with the man who owned it. I sized him up and noticed his furrowed brows and tight lips that gradually relaxed as our eyes locked.

We were both frozen in the moment. I wasn't sure what his reason for pause was, but mine had everything to do with how fine he was. But even his sexy couldn't distract me from the shit I just stepped in... or crashed into.

I dragged my eyes off him and twisted my head toward his car's bumper, mentally sobering up quick from my rage. My jaw nearly hit the ground. I smashed the back end of his car in so badly, the bumper hung off on one side.

"I am *so* sorry," I apologized to his car instead of him. My eyes zeroed in on the vehicle. A *McAlister LT*. I knew nothing about the brand, but the car appeared to be hella expensive.

My hands were in my locs when I turned to sweep my eyes his way again, to see his eyes not on mine but on my body before he snatched them off me completely.

He was so handsome. Perfectly filled in mustache and beard combo, deep brown dreamy eyes. He had the stereotypical ideal facial features of a black action figure. And his shoulders? Those joints, sat squared and broadly stacked above his back, like a basketball player's. He was tall like one too. I couldn't take notice of much else, given the situation, but judging by the tailored fit of his black wool coat and the shine of his shoes not to mention the expensive car he hopped out of, I would say, I hit the wrong fucking car that day.

I slapped both hands to my mouth to cover this time. The gentleman approached me slow, his gait almost poetic, his slightly bowed legs adding to his appeal.

"Sir, I am so sorry," I repeated to him this time without making eye contact. "I don't know what the hell that was."

I angled my eyes up at him to find his jaw a little slacked, pupils roaming all over my face.

"I wasn't paying attention. Some would say I blacked out. *Fuck*," I whispered that last part to myself. "Your car looks expensive. It looks *extremely* expensive. Shit, we'll be here forever waiting on the cops to pull up to give us a police report. Dammit, dammit, dammit, Zoe. Fuck!"

My eyes rolled up again to meet his. He looked in shock.

"Oh my goodness." I placed my hand on his arm. "I'm over here just thinking about myself. Just selfish. Are you all right? Do you need to sit down? Should I call an ambulance?"

"Uh, no, no." He shook his head as if doing so would ground him. "Are you all right?"

I pressed my hand to my chest. "I'm fine... physically. But... shit, I fucked up."

Cars drove around us. Drivers blared their horns and shouted their own set of expletives as they sped off in their vehicles.

I left his side to advance toward his car again, and my heart sank when I fully accessed the damage. This was bad. "My insurance will go way up when they hear about this." I shut my eyes while choking back a cry.

"Um, you know what?" He clapped his hands once. "We can handle this ourselves. No need to wait for the police to arrive to writeup a report."

I whipped my head in his direction so fast. My brows wrinkled next. "I'm sorry, what?"

He smiled and my heart did somersaults. "I'm also pressed for time. I can contact two tow trucks and they can tow both of our cars. I can even cover a cab for you to get to your destination."

My jaw dropped and my eyes widened to the size of saucers. Suddenly my head spun. "Are you sure you don't want for me to call an ambulance, 'cause I don't think you're thinking straight."

He chuckled.

"You do know *I* hit *you*... right?"

He offered a warm smile. "I do."

"And you want to tow *my* car?"

"That's right."

"And call *me* a cab to get home?"

"Also correct."

I moved closer to him and lifted the back of my palm to his forehead. "Are you *sure* you didn't bang your head against your steering wheel?"

He laughed a hearty laugh that made me chuckle a little myself, my brows still furrowed.

"I'm Bryant." He extended his hand to me. "And you are?"

"Zoe." I accepted his hand. "My name is Zoe Stewart, and I take full responsibility for ruining your day."

He laughed again. "It's quite fine. I'll tell you what Zoe. I'll call up a private tow truck company that will be here in a short time. After that we can exchange phone numbers and sort all of this out between us two. Once that's all taken care of, I can call you a black car and the driver will take you to wherever you were planning to get to at this hour. Does that work for you?"

All I could do was nod.

"Perfect, I'll get right on that." He turned away and pulled out his device from his pocket to place a call.

I stood there staring at him, very confused.

"Okay, what the hell just happened here?" I asked myself.

———

It was an easy decision to take that guy up on his offer. Although when I'd accepted his suggestion of paying for my cab to get me to where I was going, I thought he'd lost his mind. *I* hit *his* car, and he arranged for a black car to take *me* home? What the hell? I couldn't even remember his name. I figured I'd cross that bridge, ask him for his name again when he called me to schedule a time for us to sit down and sort the accident out between us two.

I shook my head as I sat in the backseat of that black car. It was a pretty dope one too. This was not your regular shared ride service either. This black car was a private one. An all black crisp *Tesla* with genuine leather heated seats and a driver who was kind enough to offer me bottled spring water. The gentleman I rammed into dialed the number right in front of me and requested it. Didn't even ask me where I lived, just told me to tell the driver once I was inside the car.

"Dammit, what's his name again?" I mumbled to myself.

I could have asked the guy driving me, but the nonsense I was in route to preoccupied my mind. Instead of stopping at the salon for my appointment like I'd previously planned, I rescheduled and opted to head home. I had trash at my apartment that needed throwing out immediately.

"I can't believe he has her in my home," I mumbled while fighting back tears.

My phone was in the palm of my hand. I played, then replayed the video sent to me, with the volume turned off this time. It was no doubt that little bitch recorded and texted the video to me from Rocco's phone. Why wouldn't she? She warned me and I laughed in her face, not taking her seriously.

Rocco and I had been together since I was 16-years-old and him 19-years-old. He was my first and only love. I gave that man everything, including my teenage years and my entire 20s. He knew I wanted marriage and kids, that to me was the logical next step. But here we were, fifteen years later and still no ring or a child to call my own. And now I saw the reason for the stall.

"Motherfucker," I whispered to myself as I gritted my teeth.

I had suspicions he was stepping out on me. The elders in the neighborhood who watched everything move around the block would tell me they saw him with "so and so" while I was at work. That he wasn't at the auto-shop all day where he worked as a mechanic when he claimed he was. For a time, close to two years, Rocco was on the hunt for employment. He'd lost his job driving school buses because of cutbacks. Rocco wanted work like that bus driving gig but couldn't secure one, and I was fine with that. I stood by my man, made the money and brought it home for us to divide between us while he claimed to have been searching for extra work. The old ladies around the way told me to stop being stupid, though. Insisted he was out here playing games, but I refused to believe that until I couldn't deny the change in his behavior. Eventually I wanted proof and finally got it.

The driver pulled over at the curb. I thanked him and stepped out of the black car, stomping my way to my building's lobby door.

The time between stepping on and off the elevator was such a blur. In that time, I'd unlatched my earrings and gathered my locs up to the top of my head to secure in a large bun.

I stood on the threshold of my apartment door and took several deep breaths. What I wanted to do was to storm in there like a bull in a china shop taking everything and everyone out on sight, but I really didn't want to let him get the best of me.

After my third deep breath to calm down, failed to calm me down, I mumbled, "Fuck it."

I turned my keys in their respective locks and barged inside. I'd taken only a few steps through the door when I found Miss Thang sprawled out on my couch wearing only his tee that hung on her three sizes too big. She smirked when she saw me.

"Baby?" I heard him say from the kitchen before he swaggered out to face the living room. "You want green peppers in your eggs?"

"Nah, motherfucker!" I spat behind him. "I want *you* and this bitch out of my apartment right now."

His head whipped quick in my direction. Rocco's jaw dropped and his brows shot up once he recognized me.

I observed him in only his boxers, gripping a frying pan by the silver handle. It surprised me to learn he knew how to use that thing. Rocco hadn't so much as boiled water around me.

"Oh shit," he turned for the kitchen as I made my way past it.

"*You*." I pointed at the woman I now knew to be Kali as I made my way to the bedroom. "Get the fuck out."

She was up and out of her seat. "Didn't I tell you to remember my face?"

I stopped and turned to face her. "You did. And if I have to look at you for much longer, I might rearrange that face of yours, and I promise I'll always remember it then."

"Zoe, baby," he ran out of the kitchen heading my way. "This is not what you think it is."

I turned on my heels to face him and folded my arms. "Oh no? Then what is it? Huh?! Tell me. I got time to hear this."

"She just..." His eyes rolled around the room, searching for a lie. "Kali just needed to use the computer."

"Oh! She needed to use the computer. With you only in your boxers and her wearing just your t-shirt, Rocco?!" I pulled my phone out of my back pocket to access the video message that was sent to me. I pressed play, then held the device in his view. "Are you calling your dick the computer now?"

He gasped, slapping his fist to his mouth, stepping back and turning to face her. "Yooo! What the fuck Kali?! Why would you do that?"

I fanned my hand at them both as I turned to head for the bedroom.

"You claimed you loved me. I wanted to see how true that shit was nigga!" she yelled. "You also swore you didn't want her anymore and wanted to break up. So I helped speed the breakup, up. You're welcome."

I scoffed as I pulled opened drawers and snatched out anything that belonged to him. My eyes welled with tears as I threw each garment of clothing out the door of our bedroom.

"Baby, please," he begged, running into the room, tripping over his clothes on the floor. "Look, I'm sorry. All she did was give me head."

"Liar," she challenged from the door as she buttoned her jeans. "We fucked twice this morning."

"GET OUT!" I yelled at her. "If I have to tell you again, it won't be with words."

"Rocco, let's go," she demanded, ignoring my threat.

I switched my head in his direction. "Yeah, Rocco, go. Get out! Because your ass ain't staying here with me." I moved to the closet and started pulling his stuff out of his side, the hangers spinning off the rods and clattering to the floor.

"Baby—"

I paused and turned to face him, to jab my finger against his chest. "I gave you fifteen *fucking* years and you out here humiliating me with the likes of her? HER?!"

"Zoe—"

"*This* bird of all people? For real?!"

"I'm sorry—"

"Get. The. Fuck. OUT!" I screamed and shoved him away. "I want you out."

"Quit lying. You don't mean that." He licked his lips. "You ain't going nowhere."

"You're right." I pushed past him. "*You* are."

I snatched up a few of his clothes off the floor on my way to our window. The moment I opened it, a rush of that Brooklyn winter air smacked me in the face. Five pairs of his jeans went fluttering out that window a second later.

"Yo! What the fuck are you doing?!"

"Nigga, helping you move!" I replied without glancing his way. My eyes roamed over to hers. "And what the fuck are you still doing here? You should be downstairs helping him pack."

"Rocco," she called to him, eyes still locked on mine. "Let's go. You can come and stay with me."

I grunted and punched my hand twice. "Shorty, I'm giving you five seconds to get the hell out of my face and my place before you're the next thing going out that window."

She balled her lips and pointed her eyes on Rocco.

"5... 4..." I screamed. "3... 2?.."

"Rocco, I'll meet you outside," she stated through her teeth.

I squinted my eyes at her as she stomped out.

"You foul as fuck for this," he mumbled as he dove into one of the few pair of his jeans left in the apartment.

I jabbed my index finger against my chest this time. "*I'm* foul?!"

"Putting me out because of some bitch."

"*You* put yourself out, Rocco. How could you be so damn disrespectful? In the apartment we share, you fool? Why are you not at work? All the shit I've done for you and you do this? But you have the balls to call *me* foul?"

"You always ready to throw in my face all the shit you did for me, Zoe. When does that shit end? Every time I do something you don't like, here you are telling me about all the stuff you did for me when I was out of work."

"*Rocco*," I stressed. "You just fucked another bitch in a home we shared! You can't be this stupid and selfish." I pressed my fingertips to my temples, then threw my arms in the air. "You know what? Whatever. You made your choice and I'm making mine. I'm done. I knew you were doing shit behind my back. People been warning me about your ways. I just needed to see it for myself."

"Yo, Zoe, on some real shit. You ain't never gonna do better than me, baby, believe that."

I stepped back to get a better view of him and his audacity.

He shrugged in response. "Speaking facts. You cute, got a body. But there ain't nothing else exciting about you, Zee. I've been waiting to make my exit for sometime now, to be honest."

"I wish you did me the courtesy of exiting sooner." My bottom lip trembled as I pointed behind me at the door. "Her? You fuck up all we've built together for her?"

"Man, listen..."

"All I see in you right now is the time I wasted," I whispered. "Time I will never, *ever* get back."

Rocco kissed his teeth and chucked his chin toward our bedroom. "Let me just get the rest of my stuff and I'll bounce."

"Uh-Uh." I stood in his way and refused to move. "You don't get the luxury of packing. *All* your shit is going out the window. Get them outside."

He scoffed.

"Get the fuck out of my apartment right now. And you can keep the keys because I'm calling the locksmith to change my locks right after you leave."

Rocco swallowed hard, his eyes turning dark. "You'll never find another man like me in your life."

"God, I hope not." I shot back.

His feet were in his boots and his ass was out my door seconds later. The moment I heard the door slam shut, I let my emotions, the ones I'd been holding back, bubble to the surface and finally spill out of me. My chest heaved, and I allowed gravity to take over. All strength left me as I fell to my knees and wailed into my hands.

THREE

The soft whir that stirred from my windows as the curtains automatically drew open woke me. I didn't care too much for alarm clocks. I preferred to wake with the sun. So, I programmed my curtains to slide open with the sunrise.

I blinked sleep from my eyes as I ran my fingers over the hairs of my beard.

It was a Thursday, three days after the accident, and I couldn't get her out of my head.

Zoe.

Even her name was beautiful. That woman was stunning. Earthy but sexy all the same. Growing up, I had an intense crush on Lisa Bonet. Met her twice at events around New York City and California when I traveled there, but she was much older than I was and wouldn't glance my way more than once when we crossed paths. That's who Zoe reminded me of, a younger and darker Lisa Bonet, but with beautiful brown eyes and lips that were fuller and plush. Her long locs that shimmered beneath the winter sun shone magnificently on her. They have always fascinated me on women, and hers were enchanting. The length of them was actually what helped guide my eyes down her frame. She had more curves than a highway exit.

I chuckled at the thought. Her physique was hard to miss because she wore a short puffer coat, unzipped.

I scratched my head, then ran my palm over my low cut hair. For three days, she's been on my mind and her phone number in my list of contacts. I questioned if it was a wise idea, opting out of getting a police report for the accident. I actually offered to call her a black car and pay for her ride home along with the towing of her car.

And for good reason.

Success is 50% luck and 50% preparation. The second I saw who slammed into my car, flipping sounds of cash flowing through a cash counter echoed from the corners of my mind.

She was about to give me more than her insurance could ever for my car's damages.

As if on cue, my phone rang on the wireless charger that sat on the table beside my armoire. I kept my device there at night to force myself to keep my eyes off my phone's screen and my lids closed so that I could get adequate sleep for the following day.

"Grandmother," I greeted once I answered the phone. "Good morning."

"Good morning, Bryant!" she sang. "How are you, my dear?"

"I'm well," I replied, leaning against my armoire. "Just rose for the day moments ago. Yourself?"

"I'm fabulous, Bryant, just fabulous. I'm scheduled to go on my morning walk in just a few, but I wanted to reach out to you first." She giggled. "Are we still on for this Saturday at 11:30 am? GrayArea, correct? Since you've put the little birdie in my ear about managing the Morgansville property, I'm now eager to hand that precious gem off."

"Are you?" I replied, beaming. "That's fantastic! And yes, grandmother, we are still on for Saturday."

"Excellent." She clapped in the background.

I chuckled.

"And you'll invite your lovely girlfriend as well, correct?"

"*Uh...*"

"Bryant, I *must* meet her, I beg of you. Please don't be like your cousins who introduce me to their significant others only after they've done the disservice of marrying them first. I was lucky enough for

Addison to set up a meet and greet with her fiancé, Jason, months ago, but I promise it's because she's the only girl granddaughter I have. Women are more empathetic, you know? We're natural nurturers. I swear, you boy grandchildren are impossible in matters of the heart. I don't get it! You know, in my day..."

She kept rambling as I sorted out my plan, organizing my thoughts and figuring out a way to execute everything by Saturday. The moment the metaphorical light bulb lit up over my head and everything made sense and I had a plan where everyone involved could benefit, I nodded my approval.

"Yes, grandmother," I finally interjected on her rambling, "myself and my girlfriend will be in attendance for brunch at *GrayArea*."

"Thank the most high! Oh, I'm so excited, Bryant! You've made me *so* happy. I can not *wait* to meet her."

A few minutes after I ended the call with my grandmother, I stood at my floor-to-ceiling window training my eyes on the view in front of me.

I purchased this 24,000 square foot mansion that sat on a 2-acre lot because of this view of the water. Set in Long Island, my 10-bedroom estate was truly a sight to marvel at. I'd purchased the two neighboring homes beside it and the land around them so that I could knock them down and pave the roads for my private landing strip. I also sectioned off extra land to house my private jet. A giant fence extended around the perimeter with two armed guards on the east and west ends of the estate. I had small houses built outside the gates of the property just for them.

There weren't neighbors for miles and I appreciated that, preferred it actually.

I peeked down at the phone in my hand and tapped into my contacts.

"Okay, Zoe," I said to myself. "It's time to pay off your debt."

I clicked her name and placed the phone to my ear again. The phone rang three times before she finally answered on the last ring.

"Hello?" she crowed.

Her voice sounded weighted in emotion. As if she'd been crying.

"Yes, is this Zoe Stewart?"

She cleared her throat. "This is she. Who am I speaking to?"

"Zoe, this is Bryant Greene."

My name was its own celebrity and without me trying it seemed. What with the many magazines and newspaper features I've received along the years. It was a fascinating sight seeing a black man with money, I suppose. Usually just the mention of my name sent people in a tailspin.

"I'm sorry, who?" she asked.

My brows furrowed.

"Bryant," I repeated. "Greene?"

Silence.

I jerked my head back.

"I... um." I scrubbed my brows with my fingertips. "I'm the guy you hit?"

"Oh." Suddenly she gasped. "Oh! *Oh my goodness*, right, hi!" I heard the sound of a bed creaking on her end. "How are you?"

"I'm well, yourself?"

"Honestly." She sighed. "I've had much, *much* better days."

"Hmm, is this related to the accident?"

"I wish," she whispered in a way that seemed to be more so to herself. Zoe audibly inhaled the air surrounding her and added, "Anyway, is this what this call is about? To discuss the accident and sort everything out?"

I twisted my lips to one side, my eyes moving around.

"Hello?"

"Yes, I'm here." I squeezed my eyes shut. "And yes, this *is* about the accident. Listen, I'd like for us to meet up this weekend, on Saturday at 11:30 a.m. for brunch at a place called *GrayArea*. It's in the midtown section of Manhattan. Are you familiar with it?"

"Uh, no," she disclosed. "I've never been there, but I'll find it, no problem."

"Perfect. I must ask - are there any dietary restrictions I should be aware of?"

"No, I eat just about everything, if you couldn't tell." A brief laugh echoed through the phone, her voice still weighted.

"I assure you, the meet-up won't be stressful in the least," I affirmed. "So hopefully knowing that will lift your spirits a bit."

"Hmph," she huffed. "It does a little. Okay, so I'll see you on Saturday at 11:30 a.m.?"

"Indeed you will." I smiled.

"Perfect. See you then, Brian."

My smile fell off my lips.

"It's actually—" Her ending the call abruptly made me pause in speech. "—Bryant."

I dropped my view to the phone and cocked my head to one side, perplexed. "She doesn't remember my name."

I snorted a laugh at the reality of that fact. Instead of being offended by it, though, I was intrigued.

FOUR

I inhaled the eucalyptus perfuming the air the moment I strolled into The Coral Lotus. The hour had just hit 9 a.m. when my feet touched the welcome mat. My girl Joi started working here as an esthetician and masseuse only a few months ago. She insisted I stop by to see her after what went down that Monday with Rocco and Kali. Joi had been busy lately, what with getting situated at her new job. I figured I'd meet her halfway. I needed a place to relax anyway before meeting up for brunch - with the guy I hit - later that morning.

"Hey, beautiful," she welcomed from her chair. "Take off your coat and come lie here."

I sighed as I peeled off my short puffer coat and pulled my locs up to the top of my head. "You do not understand how much I need this right now, J."

"Ma'am, I can only imagine." She patted the table in front of her. "Come and lay down and let your sis take care of you."

I lumbered my way over to the table and reclined back against it, exhaling all the air out of me.

She peered down at me and I rolled my eyes up to meet hers.

"You still crying over this fuck nigga, Zo?!" She kissed her teeth, turning for a moment to get products. "Got bags forming beneath your eyes over his punk ass. Make me want to hop on the 3 to go kick him in the balls and leave an imprint of my fist on that trick's face."

"Fifteen years, Joi," I mumbled, closing my eyes. "If it was only a few measly years, you know I wouldn't sweat it. Rocco was my first everything, you know that."

I didn't have to open my eyes to know Joi was rolling hers. She always hated him. Even before Rocco and I got together, she couldn't stand him.

As she set up the small table beside her she asked, "So you threw all his shit out the window, huh?"

"Girl, every fucking piece of item that he even touched in my apartment kissed that concrete." I smirked. "I'm not even sure if he got it all or if people came around picking through them like a thrift sale."

Joi cackled.

"Honestly, I don't even care. You should have seen his shit feathering the air, though. It was like a scene out of a Downy commercial."

"I heard he moved in with that Kali clown and her mother. Shorty doesn't even have her own crib."

I kissed my teeth. "Talkin' 'bout, *'Rocco, you can stay with me.'* He is so damn stupid. What was I doing?"

"I have no idea, but you know what? He did you a big favor."

Joi hovered a steaming machine near my face. She held the unit at a safe distance and kept going in on Rocco and Kali with no mercy.

My best friend, Joi. We'd known each other since grade school and had been tight ever since. Out of all the friends that have come into and gone out my life, my relationship with Joi has forever remained consistent. She was the neighborhood pretty girl. Gorgeous golden brown skin, big beautiful eyes, and pouty lips. She attracted men of all ages like bees to pollen. After ending a really twisted situation with a married dude, she'd shaped up and got her shit together. Joi also found a new man during all that - Jeremiah. He's a cop, a detective. Well actually he had plans to leave law enforcement any day now to focus entirely on the center he ran out of Brownsville. He was so good for her. Jeremiah was someone Joi would have never seen herself getting with. I guess dating outside the box was necessary these days to find genuine love.

She tapped me on the shoulder. "Did you hear me?"

"Huh?"

"Wait, don't tell me this fool Rocco got you spacing out on me now!"

I giggled. "Joi, hush. What did you say?"

"I asked you about this brunch you're going to after this." She laid her warm fingertips against my temples to massage. "Who are you meeting up with?"

"Oh!" I kissed my teeth. "With all this shit going on with Rocco, I forgot to tell you about my car accident."

"Car accident?!" she hollered. "What car accident?"

"So, while I was driving from Jackie's photoshoot for her bundles website, at a studio near Times Square, that video Kali sent me popped up on my phone and drove me into a fit behind the wheel. I was losing my shit in the car and accidentally slammed my foot on the gas pedal and ran into the car in front of me."

"Sis, what?!"

"Girl." I shook my head. "Anyway, the guy I hit, Brian... he offered to not have us call the police to have a report drawn up but to sort it out between us. So that's what we'll do at brunch later."

"Hmmm," she hummed. "That's... different."

"Tell me about it." I snickered. "Sis, the man offered to tow my car and called a black car to get me home although I had plans to go to the shop but after I got that video—"

"Hold on, rewind." Joi held her hand up. "You hit *him* and he offered to tow *your* car and call *you* a cab?"

"Yeah, crazy, huh?"

"He must've had money to do all that because I know if some crazy bitch slammed into the back of my car, I'm taking her for all her loot."

I pinched the side of her thigh.

"Oww!" she yelped, before bursting into giggles. "What? I'm just sayin'."

I rolled my eyes closed.

"You needed to have that old car of yours traded in, anyway. Now you can get a new one, hopefully."

"I probably won't even bother getting another car. Parking is horrible now in Brownsville."

"Word. Can't say I'm happy to be back there," Joi huffed. "But my man loves the 11212, so I gotta love her ugly ass too, I guess."

We both giggled at that.

Joi and Jeremiah's relationship was so sweet. He cared a lot about her and she adored him. They were perfect for each other.

"What kind of car was this Brian driving, anyway?"

"Girl, some *McAlister*-something model," I revealed with a laugh. "I don't really know. I'd never heard of the car brand before that day. The car was dope, though. Real sleek and silver chromed like a bullet."

"A *McAlister*?! He... he was driving a *McAlister*?"

"*Mmm-hmm.*" I closed my eyes and settled into relaxing. "You know it?"

"Wa-was it a *McAlister LT*?"

"Yeah, I think so...?"

Joi grabbed me by the shoulders and pushed me to sit up.

"Hey!" I hollered. "What?!"

Literally knocked out my zone, I immediately turned to face her. It was hard to miss her mouth that hung wide open, her bulging eyes, or her hands she held up in front of her.

"Was he American or middle eastern?"

"He was a brother."

She exhaled a trembling breath, pressing her hand to her cleavage.

I grimaced. "Girl, what is wrong with you?"

She waved my question off. "What did you say his name was again?"

"Brian," I answered, "why?"

"Brian or *Bry-ant*?"

I wrinkled my brows. "I think, Brian. Why would it be Bryant? Isn't that like a last name? Why would his first name be a last name?"

Joi was out of her seat.

"What?" I questioned out loud. "Where are you going? I was really getting into that temple massage."

"A *McAlister* is an exclusive luxury vehicle," she informed, in front of her purse, which she began rummaging through.

"Okay...?"

"I remember reading this article in *For The Culture* about this car that cost upward of $200 million. A *McAlister LT*."

"Damn, $200 million? For a car?!"

"There are only three *McAlister LTs*... in the *entire* world, Zoe."

"Oh-kay...?"

"Only two people own it. This prince in the middle east owns two of them, and the other one is owned by a black guy here in the U.S."

Her attention was back in her purse, which she now turned over to empty the contents out of.

"What are you looking for?"

"My damn phone," she answered, turning to face me with it. "Got it!"

Joi typed in a few things, fanning herself in the process as if she were trying to calm herself down. Finally, she turned the device to face me. "Was this the guy?"

I squinted at the photo, observing it. In the photo was a brown skin gentleman with deep brown eyes, smooth brown skin and a smile that made my heart skip beats.

"Hmph, yeah, Brian." I pointed at the screen. "That's a wonderful photo of him—"

"Noooo!" she stage whispered loud, an enormous smile pulling at her lips. "*This* man is Bryant Greene."

"Okay...?"

"*The* Bryant Greene."

I shrugged my shoulders and shook my head, still lost. "Okay, yeah, you're going to have to help me out with this one sis because I don't have a clue who this man is—"

"Multi-billionaire Bryant Greene."

I dipped my chin. "Billionaire?"

"*Multi*-billionaire. Which means he has not just one billion but many." Joi was out of her seat pacing in front of me. "He owns mad dinner theaters. Jeremiah took me to one of them on our first date. It's gorgeous, absolutely beautiful!"

I watched her from my incline on the bench.

"He lives in this big ass mansion in Long Island. Sis, the land and his crib are *so* big. So colossal, he needed his own zip code."

Joi stopped in front of me and said, "And that fine ass wealthy man wants you."

I burst into hearty laughter. "Girl, how you figure that?!"

She pulled her chair closer to the bench and dropped herself into it. "You hit his car, slammed into the back of it. The accident was all your fault, no question about that. He not only offers to tow your car, but he calls a black car to pick you up and take you home at no charge to you? Think Zo." She flicked me on my temple.

"Ow, Joi! Why you always gotta be so violent?!"

"Think!" she repeated, her eyes lit with excitement.

I jerked my head back. "But, why? Why would he want... me?"

She squealed in front of me while dancing in her seat. "Oh my God, my best friend has landed herself the baller of all ballers!"

My eyes were moving all over the room.

"Talk about an upgrade from that loser Rocco, whew! I can't wait to throw that in his face!" Joi yanked me into a tight hug, then pulled away.

"Look, forget about this basic ass facial you asked me to give you." Joi was out of her seat and in her silver case, placing a bunch of vials and jars on the counter. "I'm about to give you the platinum experience for your platinum baller. You got to be glowing at this brunch later." She turned to glance my way and did a double take. "You gonna be wearing that?!"

I peeked down at my chunky black sweater, black skinny jeans, and booties, and nodded.

Joi shrugged. "Whatever. You're beautiful so you'll pull it off. Besides, he fell for you as you are. Girl, your wedding will be fire!" She did a little dance, then started jumping in place. "My best friend hooked a baller, ahhhh! I am too hyped for you! Wait until I tell Jeremiah."

As she continued to go on and on about Bryant's resume, painting some fictional fairytale ending involving him and I, all I could pay attention to was the little voice in my head questioning, "What does a billionaire want with me?"

FIVE

I waited outside the doors of GrayArea. My grandmother was a huge fan of this restaurant. Even suggested that I find out how I could buy into the business. Perhaps finance the opening in another location. Restaurants were a tricky investment, the only investment I've done well with avoiding. The overhead, the expenses. It was a high in-demand business, New Yorkers loved dining out, but consistency wasn't a strong suit of most restaurants that weren't high-end.

"Sir?" I heard behind me.

When I glanced over my shoulder, I spotted my head security guard, Paul standing tall behind me.

"We have two men set up on both corners inside the restaurant," he explained. "Carl and I can park ourselves one table over from yours—"

"That won't be necessary, Paul." I slid my phone out of my wool coat's pocket to check the time. "It will not be one of those meetings. This is just brunch with a... client," I said, nodding. "Yes, a client and my grandmother. Pretty tamed."

I moved my eyes around the street outside the restaurant. "And the area doesn't seem too much of a concern at this hour. You and Carl can be on the opposite ends of where your other men are, and I think that will be fine."

Security had become a must in public settings after a feature about me appeared in the local newspaper. Everyone didn't recognize me, but the ones who did liked to approach in droves, raising concerns for my safety.

"Not a problem, sir," Paul replied. "Should I wait out here with you?"

"I'll be fine alone."

I turned to face forward and spotted her making her way to the crosswalk to cross the street.

"My appointment has just arrived." A smile pulled at my lips. "You can head in."

"Will do." Paul opened the restaurant's door and disappeared inside.

She wore a short puffer coat – the same one I met her in - over an all black attire. A wool sweater peeked below the coat's hem, draping just past the belt loops of her black jeans. Her strut offered sneak peeks of her hips and ass from the front. I licked my lips at her locs that shimmered beneath the sun. I'd never seen locs so shiny before. They sparkled on her.

A smile appeared on her lips the closer she approached. In front of me, I towered over her, causing her to tilt her head back a bit to meet my eyes.

"Good morning, Zoe," I greeted.

"Good morning." She peeked behind me. "This place is fancy, huh?"

"Oh, it's actually not."

Her eyes fell to her attire, then rolled up to examine mine. Like a moving pin, Zoe traced my figure with those same eyes. "I hope there isn't a dress code."

"There isn't. GrayArea is really just a low-key spot for the lunch and after-work crowd." I rubbed my hands together. "They just offer great brunches and drinks."

She pointed her chin to the door. "So... shall we?"

"Before we do." I forced a smile. "I have a proposition for you."

She folded her arms immediately and balanced some of her bodyweight on one hip. "Proposition?"

"My grandmother..." I pointed behind me with my thumb. "... is here today. She insisted on meeting up for brunch while she's in town."

"Okay... so should we reschedule?"

"Not necessary."

She stared at me. "So you plan for us to discuss the accident in front of your grandmother?"

"We will discuss the accident right now." I gestured with my head for her to follow me two feet away from the restaurant's entrance. "Zoe, I'm willing to forget all about the accident."

She cocked a brow when I stopped and turned to face her again.

"I'll even offer to buy you a new vehicle, whichever one of your choosing."

"If?" she asked

"*If.*" I chuckled nervously, while examining her reaction, aware of how crazy the next thing I planned to say would sound to her. But I went for it, anyway. "If you pretend to be my girlfriend for the next hour or so."

Zoe tilted her head to one side, brows slowly wrinkling in confusion. After a moment of saying nothing, she laughed while holding a hand up. "I'm sorry, *what*?"

I adjusted the collar of my coat and leaned my back against the restaurant's brick wall. "My grandmother in there loves, love. She was a matchmaker in her youth and she adores seeing her grandchildren in relationships," I lied. To be honest, my grandmother truly loved love, and she really liked to see her grandchildren in flourishing commitments, but that was not at all my reason for asking Zoe to play pretend with me.

When she hit my car in Times Square, a lightbulb went off. She was beautiful, yes, but she had entered my life at the most opportune time. I told my grandmother I had a girlfriend so she would eagerly give me the property sort to say, and a "girlfriend" kind of materialized. Zoe didn't need to hear that part, though.

"My friend clued me in on who you are."

I blinked twice. "Oh, did they?"

"Yeah," she answered. "I don't follow the who's who the way she does, so it wasn't clear who I was dealing with until earlier this morning."

"And what did your friend tell you?"

"Enough to make it glaringly obvious that you asking me to do this is odd as hell, but especially for a man like you."

I laughed. "It's out of the ordinary, I'll admit."

She gave me a once-over. "Like, do you own a mirror? You're not only wealthy, you're *very* good looking."

I smiled, really I blushed. I'd heard this before, but coming from her, it kind of held more weight. "Thank you."

"Oh, but you're aware." She smirked. "You can ask any other woman to pretend to be your girlfriend. *Why* on earth are you asking *me*?"

"Because you'll do anything I ask you to do in this very moment and I can have more control over the situation and you because of that," was what I wanted to say.

Zoe was right. It would seem like I could easily ask any other woman to play pretend with me for an hour, but I wanted *her*. Besides me having the upper hand in this deal, the one thing Zoe had that I hadn't seen anywhere else was how real and likable she was. She was gorgeous in a non-flashy kind of way. Like a diamond in the rough. There was a lot more to her than the pool of women I could choose from. Tack on the normal vibe she gave off in my presence, making me feel like, I don't know, a regular person in the company of a woman for once, comforted me. She hardly remembered my name, which meant she expected nothing from me and was least likely to take advantage of the situation. This allowed her to be herself, and that was appealing. *Really* appealing.

"I'm asking you because I see how we both can benefit from this, that's why." I folded my hands in front of me. "You hit *me*, remember?"

She smiled and my heartbeat hammered.

"And I'm not interested in penalizing you for that," I made known. "It would be absurd for me to ask you to pay for the damages on my car."

"I heard your car cost you $200 million and is an extremely exclusive find."

"Yes." I leaned inward. "You slammed into a very expensive car."

She giggled nervously.

"But we don't have to dwell on that. An hour or so, just be my companion. After the allotted time, we'll forget all about the accident and I'll finance your new car. I'll even have it delivered right to your doorstep. Just tell me what you want and it's done."

Her eyes darted across my face and I licked my lips slow, a bit concerned with the delay in reply.

She flipped a few locs over her shoulder. "Okay. I'd be a fool to turn a deal like this down. So fine, I'll be your *girlfriend* for an hour or so."

"Excellent." I turned to head toward GrayArea's entrance. "Let's just head—"

"Wait, hold up." She grabbed my arm.

I turned to examine her grip, then moved my eyes to meet hers.

"If we plan to be boyfriend and girlfriend for an hour or so," she stated with finger quotes, "We should learn a few things about each other first, don't you think?"

I squinted my eyes waiting for her to continue.

"You're a stranger to me. I just learned today that your name isn't Brian but Bryant," she revealed.

"Ah, yes. I recall you referring to me as Brian the other day."

"Exactly. And grandmother's be knowing." She smiled. "So we have to at least memorize the basics about each other and have our story in order. When is your birthday?"

"April 24th."

"Mine is August 25th. Where did you grow up?"

"The Hamptons."

"Of course." She snorted a laugh, then pointed at herself. "Brooklyn, Brownsville."

"I should have asked you this before," I intoned, "but do you have a boyfriend?"

Her smile fell as she slightly turned her head away to hide her frown.

"I mean, not that it matters," I offered. "As I've said, this is only for an hour. You are not expected to do anything—"

"I don't have a boyfriend... anymore."

I could tell there was a story there, but I refused to probe considering the time constraint. The question was geared more toward satisfying my curiosity, anyway.

"And I'm assuming you're single?" she countered.

"I haven't had a relationship since my early 20s."

Her brows shot up. "How old are you?"

"33 yourself?"

"I just turned 31. You're 33 and you haven't had a relationship since your 20s?"

"I've been a little busy."

Building an empire that's about to get even bigger with your cooperation.

I turned to peek at the entrance. "We should head in now. My grandmother has been waiting for sometime. Are we all caught up?"

"Yeah, I guess so... um, are you sure I'm dressed right for this?"

My eyes moved about her frame, coasting down her curves. She wasn't the stick thin women I was used to seeing at the office or out and about within my circles. Zoe had a body made for love.

"Bryant?"

"Yes." I shook my head to refocus. "What you have on is fine. As I've said, there's no dress code. Let's head in."

I led the way inside the restaurant and toward the table where my grandmother sat waiting. Our eyes met, and she smiled. Her phone was to her ear, which she lowered the moment I was steps away from the table.

"Grandmother," I announced, stepping to the side and gesturing at Zoe. "This is my girlfriend, Zoe Stewart. Zoe, my grandmother, Estelle Bryant."

Zoe's face lit up as she moved to my grandmother. She surprised me and my grandmother by leaning forward and wrapping her arms around my grandmother's shoulders.

Her commitment to the role impressed me.

"Oh!" my grandmother exclaimed, pressing her hand to Zoe's forearm in their embrace. "Aren't you sweet?"

"It's nice to meet you," Zoe made known with a smile as she stepped out of their hug. "Your last name is Bryant?"

"Yes," my grandmother beamed. "My married name. My late husband was *the* George Bryant. Bryant's mother, my daughter, insisted on giving Bryant his grandfather's surname as his first name."

"That is so interesting." Zoe's eyes moved off my grandmother's then onto mine before she took in her surroundings. "This place is nice."

I pulled out the chair beside me and said, "You can sit here."

My heart was honestly beating a thousand times a minute. I really did not know Zoe other than what she told me about herself outside. I hoped like hell she wasn't crazy and that I didn't make a deal with a lunatic.

Perhaps this wasn't the wisest idea after all.

Zoe removed her coat and draped it on the back of her chair along with her bag. With her body in full view, I realized God invested a little extra time in creating her.

Zoe turned to me and did a double take. "What?"

"Nothing," I replied.

She leaned in and whispered. "Is my outfit *that* inappropriate?"

"No," I whispered back. "It isn't inappropriate at all. You look great."

"Oh, you two are divine," my grandmother gushed across from us. "This little whisper thing you're doing is too cute."

Zoe cleared her throat and straightened her posture. I noticed when her attention dropped to the plates and utensils. "There are a lot of forks and spoons on this table."

My grandmother laughed, and I forced out a chuckle.

I leaned in closer to her and whispered, "Just follow my lead."

"So," my grandmother started, "I have to be honest with you, Zoe. When my Bryant here said *girlfriend*, I was expecting a glamazon dripping in jewels and wrapped in fur with an attitude I'd need to adjust to. But you?" She cheesed. "We've only been in each other's company but for a few minutes and I can tell you are *not* that. I'd say you have *never, ever* been that. It's a pleasant surprise to see he isn't so full of himself to catch the eye of a woman as down to earth as you."

I lifted the glass of water in front of my lips to take a sip. An interrogative question was coming, I could just feel it.

"Speaking of which - how did the two of you meet?"

Damn, I thought to myself. Can we order first?

"We uh..." I swallowed my water hard. Out of all the things Zoe and I discussed outside, how was this not one of them? "Well..."

"I bumped into him in Times Square," Zoe interjected, glancing at me. Below the table she patted my thigh, reassuringly. "Our first meeting was a hit, so we just had to exchange numbers."

I snorted a laugh and Zoe giggled.

"Aww, love at first sight! Ooooh, I love it! Isn't insta-love the absolute best? That's what you kids are calling it these days, right? You know Bryant, I met your grandfather that way." She blushed. "I'll tell you two all about it. But first, let's order. Bryant, you know how I can go on and on and I'd hate for us three to starve before I could get to the best part of my story."

Brunch proceeded at the same speed. My grandmother asking questions about our relationship and us making things up as we went along. Zoe was quite the conversationalist, very comfortable in her own skin and quick on her toes.

An hour progressed to two. My grandmother ate up the last of her lunch along with all that Zoe and I were pretending to be. Things were moving smoother than expected.

"Oh Bryant, about the property," my grandmother said as we finished up, "I'm having the paperwork notarized as we speak. I'll have them faxed to your office by Monday. Does that work?"

"It works excellently, grandmother."

"Zoe," my grandmother spoke again, "Bryant here has offered to manage this old property in Morgansville for me. Isn't that so sweet of him? I'd forgotten all about the old thing until my loving grandson mentioned it."

"Morgansville," Zoe repeated. "I've heard of that town. It's one of the oldest majority black towns in Upstate New York. A lot of the freed slaves migrated there from the south in the late 1800s."

"Yes," my grandmother confirmed, her eyes becoming big before shifting over to mine. "A young woman who understands her history. I am very impressed."

Zoe snickered. "You own property there, Mrs. Bryant?"

"I do! It's a property passed down for generations. It's almost a keep-sake of sorts."

"That's beautiful." Zoe turned to face me. "And that really is sweet that you're taking on the responsibility of managing something that's like a family heirloom."

I forced a smile. "Well, thank you."

The sparkle in Zoe's eyes when she said that almost made me feel bad about the plans I had for the property... almost.

"Zoe, will you be in attendance at Bryant's cousin Addison's wedding on New Year's Eve?"

Zoe turned to glance at me before returning her attention on my grandmother. "Um..."

"You must attend, Zoe, you simply must!"

I cleared my throat. "Uh, grandmother—"

"I will not accept you not being there." My grandmother reached her hand across the table to Zoe. "You are such a sweet, sweet woman. I can't imagine Bryant attending the festivities without his new girlfriend. There's so many people to meet and so many great things about you to show off."

Zoe switched her head in my direction with panic in her eyes.

"Zoe will be there," I insisted with a nod of finality. "We'll both be there."

"*Huh?*" Zoe whispered.

I winked at her and she cocked a brow.

"Splendid!" my grandmother clapped. "Well you two, I have an appointment with my stylist who's helping me find something to don for the wedding. I'm so excited to see you again in Long Island, Zoe."

My grandmother slid her chair back, and I stood from my seat and moved to her side of the table to lift her coat off the back of her chair.

"Oh, thank you, sweetheart." She poked her arms through each sleeve. "Always so thoughtful."

I smiled.

"Zoe," my grandmother said as she made her way over to Zoe. "It was an absolute pleasure meeting you today. You do not understand how much I've enjoyed your company."

Zoe stood up and wrapped her arms around my grandmother. I couldn't help but to notice my grandmother close her eyes in Zoe's embrace. Grandmother really liked her.

Shit.

"I swear dear, you give amazing hugs."

"Thank you, Mrs. Bryant. I appreciate that."

My grandmother stood in front of me next to give me two air kisses. "So I'll see you two on New Year's Eve. Ciao!"

I'd taken my seat beside Zoe again once we were alone to find her staring into me.

"Bryant?"

"Name your price."

"Excuse you?!"

I glanced around the room and leaned in. "Everyone has one and I'm sure you do too. *What* is your price? How much will it cost for you to accompany me to my cousin's wedding and to keep up this charade?"

She scoffed while leaning back in her seat and folding her arms. "The nerve."

"I'm not trying to offend you. This wasn't the plan, but as you can see, my grandmother has taken a liking to you."

"Grandmothers like me," she remarked, finally allowing a grin to pull at her lips. "It's my thing. But I don't want to get paid to go with you somewhere. Makes me feel like some kind of escort, which I am *not*, thank you."

I stared at her. "So, what you're saying is...?"

"I don't have a price. I'll go with you," she agreed. "Your grandmother is sweet and this thing you're doing for her, managing such an important property that means so much to her? You seem to be a good guy. So if you need the favor of me attending a wedding and pretending to be your girlfriend there too, I can do that. No biggie. Besides, if the food is as good there as it is here, I'm the real winner."

My fingers stroked the hairs on my beard and I leaned my head forward. "At least let me cover the expense of you getting to my home so we can head to the wedding. I'll also pay for your outfit for the event."

"Oh, you most definitely will cover that because the way your grandmother was sitting here dressed like a million bucks and you looking triple that, there's no way I can wear what I got in my closet."

I smiled. "No worries. I'll have all of that covered."

———

"It wasn't a date," I said into the phone. "It was brunch with my grandmother."

"So," Lennox started. "You're already taking her to meet the family."

I laughed and so did he.

"I can't believe you lied to your grandmother about you having a girlfriend."

"Says the guy who had a baby with his best friend because they agreed to a pact while they were drunk."

"Oh, touché, touché," Lennox conceded before bursting into a boisterous laugh.

It was later that evening. After parting ways with Zoe following brunch, I returned to the office for a bit to update the buyers interested in my grandmother's property. The numbers these men were throwing out made me see nothing but dollar signs. Everything was coming together nicely.

"How does she look?" Lennox asked.

"Who, Zoe?"

"Nah, your grandmother. Because I'm so interested in what granny looks like."

I laughed.

Lennox and I met a few years ago when we were both in our 20s. He'd signed with the *NBA* a few years prior, and I needed a fresh face for my sneaker cleaning business. The demographic for the business were teens and young adults, and buzz about him was building fast. So, I reached out to him. We met up for lunch, and instead of having a business meeting, we just talked like two old friends. I signed him to a $2 million endorsement deal and every time we got around each other it was always good times. We continued a friendship after we handled business and we've been friends ever since.

"Zoe's beautiful," I answered. "She's short, petite but her body." I blew air out of my mouth. "She's got the kind of curves women pay a lot of money to have, but I doubt she's had work done."

"Curvy is real nice," Lennox added.

"You know who she reminds me of?"

"Who?"

"A new millennium, Lisa Bonet. She's got the locs and the vibe, just a few shades darker. Stunning."

Lennox exhaled into the phone. "Lisa Bonet *is* bad."

"*That* she is."

"Ah, come on, man!" Lennox hollered next. "Pass the ball!"

"Who's playing?" I asked.

"The Spurs and the Ballers."

"Pryce Williams just signed on with the *Bronx Ballers*, right?"

"Yup, and he's killing it."

I leaned off the side of my bed, angling my hand for the remote on my night table. The second I clicked the button, my flat screen rose out of the built-in TV cabinet that sat at the foot of my circular bed.

"Man, I told you the team would improve with new players," Lennox reminded. "The Ballers needed that power boost. It's gold from here on out."

I switched on the TV and navigated to Channel 7 to watch the game myself.

The Ballers had been a team I've had my eyes on for a while. The cost of the team was lower than the average $1.9 billion, making it a perfect time to buy in. I'm always in search of ways to spread out my investments in different arenas and add to my business portfolio. Entertainment was a sector I'd been interested in throwing my hat into more.

"They're playing more uniformed on the court than they did when I viewed the game from the sky box two years ago."

"They are," Lennox replied. "I see rings in their future. I'm telling you, Bryant, the Ballers might be your next investment. Pryce is representing, just like I predicted he would."

"Hmph." I raised my hand to my chin to stroke the hairs of my beard. I watched as Pryce dropped not one but two balls in the net in less than a two-minute interval. The score on the clock had the Ballers leading by ten points. If he continued this way, the finals would be an actual goal worth meeting and the second they brought the trophy home, the price for the team would go up. "I'm definitely intrigued by the prospect."

"I'm excited," Lennox said next. "They invited me to watch the game from floor seats. I might just accept the invite if they keep playing the way they're playing tonight."

"I might just seriously consider really buying the team if they keep playing like how they're playing right now."

Lennox laughed. "B, hold on one second, Rylee just walked in."

Rylee and Lennox's relationship was one I've always admired and one that has confused me too. They were friends, genuinely just friends, but a year prior the two agreed to have a baby together. It was an odd arrangement, but because of their friendship and how close they were, it seemed to work.

. I heard the two of them exchanging words in the background, their voices coming in as low rumbles through the phone. My eyes drifted over to my TV again as I watched the Ballers move about the court as if they were truly finals bound. Pryce Williams previously played for the *Oakland Flames*, one of the NBA's championship teams. They'd won a ring just one year prior, and many credited the Flames' success to Pryce.

I reached for my business cellphone and held down the home button. "Siri, please remind me to ask Chelsea to gather the Ballers' stats for review on Monday."

"Bryant," Lennox said into the phone. "I have to go."

"Oh, no problem. When you have the availability, we should meet up for lunch and you can school me on the Ballers' stats from last..."

Lennox cut my speech short by ending the call.

"... year," I finished. I arched a brow at the phone. "Must have been important."

I shrugged, clicking out of my phone app. I palmed the phone for a moment when thoughts of Zoe surfaced. Thoughts of what she was doing at that hour and if she was thinking about me the way I was thinking of her.

I shook my head from side to side, hoping it would help shake my sudden preoccupation with her.

"My involvement with her is only for business," I told myself. "I am not to make this anything more."

SIX

I smiled at neighbors as I made my way up my block headed to my apartment building. It seemed like everyone clutched the handles of store shopping bags that afternoon.

With only two days left before Christmas, many people in the neighborhood were in the Christmas spirit. Christmas lights glittered at building windows. Overhead, hanging from the tops of traffic light poles, were lit decorations and fake garland signaling loud and clear we were right at the epicenter of the holiday season. The neighborhood shops blasted all kinds of Christmas music. Your typical Mariah Carey "All I Want For Christmas Is You" was an undeniable staple, but then there were the Christmas songs sprinkled with soul like "Silent Night" by The Temptations and here and there the Caribbean versions of those tracks.

I inhaled the air and smiled at the energy in the atmosphere. Christmas wasn't really my holiday, but I loved the happy-go-lucky spirit that reigned supreme during the holidays. My favorite holiday was New Year's Eve, and this year I'd be spending it with a billionaire.

I giggled to myself as I turned the corner. Never would I have imagined this being my life. Forming an arrangement with someone who apparently played with more money in a day than I have seen in a lifetime. Bryant didn't seem uppity in the least either. I mean, he spoke proper and definitely didn't cut corners with his appearance. Everything about the man seemed well-curated, and that fact impressed me. All in all, he seemed like a regular person and not like someone worth so much. I still hadn't wrapped my head around what it was he wanted with me though.

"I probably should have named my price," I mumbled to myself.

Steps away from the lobby door of my building, I heard, "Zoe," behind me.

I turned to the voice and did a double take, my lip slowly hiking up on one side.

Rocco came swaggering up the block, dressed in a heavy bubble coat, pulling up his dark-washed jeans by the belt loops when he got closer.

"What do you want Rocco?"

He licked his lips slowly in front of me and allowed a smile to push his cheeks back. "How you doin' baby?"

I didn't respond, only cocked a brow, waiting on a reply to my question.

"I came through to check you."

"For?"

"Listen, I've given you an entire week to cool off."

I took a step back to get a good view of him.

"It's cold out here." He paused to blow into his hands. "And I'm ready to come home, baby."

"Let me guess... Shit ain't as sweet or *warm* staying at Kali's mother's apartment?"

He sucked his teeth. "See, I think it's wild you're allowing someone to come between you and me."

"*You...*" I jabbed my finger into the chest of his down jacket. "... allowed someone to come between you and me."

"So, wait," He folded his arms. "You're legit not gonna let me come home? You gonna end all those years just like that? Over some bitch?"

"You know what?" I turned to push my key into the lock. "I'm not

even about to get into this with you. Explaining myself to you is stupid."
I turned to face him again and pointed. "*You* fucked up. I don't owe you
a damn thing, much less an explanation as to why I put you out. It's
abundantly clear why you had to go, Rocco."

"Baby, it was only sex, yo! I don't love Kali like I love you. You know
that. You know, can't no other female replace you."

"Oh, so they can just suck your dick under my roof, and fuck twice,
right?"

He grunted while dropping his head back between his shoulders.
"Y'all females always saying y'all want a king and that y'all queens and
shit. Sometimes the king has a few on the side, but that doesn't mean
any of them can ever take your place."

"If you don't get the fuck out of my face with your bullshit. I've
heard enough." I shook my head. "You hurt me, Rocco. And before you
did what you did, you had to understand you would hurt me too. So
what would that make me if I take you back?"

"A good woman," he replied. Rocco moved in even closer, his eyes
still on mine. His hand caressed the side of my cheek and I couldn't help
my eyes from closing after feeling his touch again. He added, "You'd be
in love with a man who loves you."

I'd known Rocco from the time I was a teenager. I birthed our relationship from grief. Now that I think about it, I never really gave myself
the opportunity to genuinely experience being *in* love. I wouldn't say I
settled, but I definitely hadn't reviewed all my other options. Yet and
still, I knew being with him was no longer an option I could live with
wholeheartedly.

"Rocco, it's over."

He sucked his teeth and stepped back from me. I noticed his attitude switched with the finality in my tone. He balled his lips, moving
around his jaw as he stared at me.

"It ain't like you gon' do better, you know that right?"

I jerked my head back.

"I'm the best thing that ever happened to you, Zoe."

"Well that lets me know I set the bar way low in the gutter if you're
the best thing to happen to *me*, huh?"

"Ain't no nigga out here gonna want a hood rat."

"Hood rat?!" I hollered.

"Yeah, baby." He licked his lips, menacingly slow, not at all seductively. "The sex was bomb, you're a giver, I'll give you that. But that's all you good for and what you'll ever be worth, ma. Just face it - you dull, Zoe. Your conversations are wack, sweetheart. Probably because you had nobody to teach you how to provide anything besides wet pussy, being a foster kid and all."

"Wow, Rocco," I exhaled, tears brimming my eyes. "That's fucking low, even for you."

He shrugged. "Just speaking facts. You boring, always have been. You like talking about shit that's..."

"Enterprising? Things that are about shit and not shallow as fuck and a waste of energy?"

He scoffed. "Stimulate a man's interest as much as you do his dick."

My phone in my back pocket buzzed with a text, but I ignored it.

"Yeah, and your interests were always about cars, money, and jewels. I'm sorry I didn't find interest in that."

"Like I said, dull."

I scoffed. "The day I caught you with that girl, you revealed you'd been waiting for the right time to bounce. So bounce. What you doin' back here?"

"Figured, I'd come to check if you came to your senses yet. It's clear you haven't."

I fanned my hand in the air as if I were shooing away a stray dog. "Goodbye Rocco. You've said what you've said, now go and stay gone, please."

He scoffed out a laugh as he backed away and left.

I made my way up to my apartment and pressed my back to the closed door once I was inside.

"What the fuck was I thinking?" I asked myself.

My phone buzzed again with a text. This time I dipped my hand into my back pocket.

Bryant:

Zoe, I've scheduled an appointment for you to meet with my

stylist, Teagan Roman, for Thursday at 11 a.m. Call me when you get an opportunity so I can send you the additional details.

I smiled.

Bryant: Also, I hope your day was well.

My eyes were down on my phone as I reread Bryant's texts. "If I'm so dull and boring, what does this man want with me?"

SEVEN

"**Y**our time," I voiced into the air, "What is it in Geneva, Torrence?"

"It's 1:45 pm at this hour," Torrence answered. "Clear blue skies, green trees surrounding me. Christmas here was a dream."

"Hmph," I huffed, leaning back in my leather chair.

On a Friday morning, two days after the Christmas holiday, I sat in my office with my desk phone on speaker, hoping to gather more details on Morgansville. Learning of the plans was a right-place-right-time kind of thing. Overheard a conversation while on the golf course a few weeks prior. The impending plans seemed financially beneficial, so I just had to throw my hat in that ring.

"So, Greene," Sam, another one of my potential buyers said on the call, "how's the acquisition coming along?"

Sam was referring to my grandmother's property in Morgansville that I may have promised I'd be able to secure for him and Torrence... at a price, a really enticing price. $2.3 billion enticing. Not only was I selling them the property, I'd even negotiated an offer for the land that surrounds it.

The property in Morgansville sat on a large 1,421 acre farm. There was enough space to plant, grow, harvest crops, and raise cattle. It was a goldmine.

"Progressive," I answered. "The papers for the property are being drawn up right now. I'm thinking by the end of this month, the property should be ready for our deal, gentleman."

"Excellent," Torrence said into the phone, adding a bit of a chuckle with his response. "The sooner we can secure that property, the better. We want to start construction on two condominiums in Q1 of 2020. And your property would be the perfect location for another development, a mixed use building perhaps."

"Hmm," I hummed. "Sounds promising."

"Oh it is," Sam chimed in next. "Morgansville is such a lovely town. The area is filled with farms, so there is a slew of open spaces to play with. From research, I see that most farmers are forfeiting their land and relocating to the city. Their children have become adults and not many millennials are interested in continuing the family farming business, which is great for us. Morgansville will do well as a metropolis outside of NYC, anyway. We're thinking about marketing it as the next Brooklyn."

"Brooklyn?" I questioned.

"Why, yes," Sam continued. "Since we're considering adding condominiums and mixed use spaces, we want to keep that city appeal and borrow from the urban culture already established in Morgansville. A *different* millennial crowd who want to live the city life but like the edge of living amongst the urban culture will find the town appealing."

"I see." I gritted my teeth. The way he kept saying urban culture, when I'm sure what he wanted to say was black, rubbed me raw. I needed to end the call before my annoyance became evident. "Well, gentleman, let's talk in the new year to square everything away."

"Perfect," Sam agreed.

"Sounds like a plan to me, Greene," Torrence answered next. "We'll speak then."

After ending the call with the investors, I leaned back in my office chair, swiveled it to my right, and stared out of my window.

Morgansville was a town I was only familiar with through my parents. Though my grandmother grew up on the property, there really wasn't much talk about Morgansville as a whole.

From what I understood, Morgansville was a predominantly black residential village, only twenty minutes outside of New York City.

The residents maintained the area as best they could. Nothing really happened in Morgansville that was worth mentioning. But the proximity to the city paired with the open space and quiet environment would definitely attract a certain crowd. Specifically, a white demographic equipped with disposable incomes.

I tucked my lips in my mouth when I thought about what this would mean if I sold the property. I've seen gentrification happen right before my eyes. Witnessed the sweeping change of neighborhoods once construction started on just one building in the area.

"$2.5 billion, though," I whispered to myself.

With the sale of my grandmother's Morgansville property, I'd be the youngest multi-billionaire in the country with a net worth of almost $10 billion.

I blew air out of my mouth and smiled at that prospect.

Without thinking, I brushed the pad of my thumb back and forth over my ring finger, the one with the dollar sign tatted on it.

I'd gotten the tattoo after a woman I dated accused me of thinking about money too much. She criticized me for being emotionally unavailable and suggested I just marry money since I paid it so much more attention.

I chuckled to myself.

I transmuted the insult into a compliment, and it's been my motto ever since.

"Sir?" a voice streamed from my cordless phone's dock.

"Yes, Chelsea?"

"Your scheduled final tuxedo fitting is in one hour. Will you be able to make it?"

"Yes," I answered, peeking down at my watch. "Is there anything else on my calendar before then?"

"All clear," she replied.

"Perfect. I can head to the tailor in the next half an hour. Have the car waiting outside for me."

"Will do, Mr. Greene."

The fitting reminded me of Zoe. I'd told her I would arrange for my stylist to assist her with scouting prospective pieces for the wedding.

"One other thing."

"Sir?"

"Has Teagan been in touch with Zoe Stewart?"

"Yes," Chelsea answered. "They're all squared away, sir. Teagan confirmed that Zoe has made her selection for the evening. Teagan even complimented on how easy of a client Zoe was."

"Yes." I smiled, pleased. "That sounds very much like Ms. Stewart."

Chelsea chuckled. "Will that be all, Mr. Greene?"

I twisted my mouth to one side and bit inside of my lip for a moment before I replied, "Would you be able to get her on the phone?"

"Who, sir?"

"Ms. Stewart."

There was a brief pause on the line until Chelsea said, "Absolutely, Mr. Greene. Right away. Please hold."

Even through the phone, I could sense the smile pulling at Chelsea's lips.

She's never asked me about my marital status, but she has dropped hints that my lack of a love life concerned her. I've known Chelsea since my mid-20s. She was five years older than me and an incredible executive assistant who managed my calendar as if it were her own. Once she asked if she should schedule any evening dates since I had an open calendar for the weekend and I declined.

"Mr. Greene," she started. "I hear stepping away from your desk and mingling a bit can be beneficial to business."

"I'm not interested in swimming in a dating pool, Chelsea. There are better things to do with my time."

"Yes, of course, sir."

That was the first and last time that conversation ever occurred, but I'm sure in the corners of her mind, she's been waiting to hear my interest pique in something other than my businesses.

"Sir," Chelsea returned on the line. "Ms. Stewart is on hold. Transferring her over now."

"Thank you, Chelsea." I adjusted the knot on my tie. "Zoe?"

"Yeah, I'm here."

Her voice was like an angel's song. Soft and angelic, almost ethereal. She spoke well but still had that tinge of inner-city that worked in her favor. It was sexy.

"Good morning," I greeted. Couldn't help the smile that pulled at my lips when I did it. "I hope I didn't disturb you or wake you."

She moaned a little on the line and blood rushed straight to my dick, a feeling I hadn't experienced in a while.

"Sorry," she said, just above a whisper. "I was stretching."

"My apologies," I growled before clearing my throat. "My apologies for waking you. I just wanted to make sure you were all set for Long Island."

"Yeah," she confirmed. "My dress and heels are secure. Teagan was amazing. I wanted to keep her."

I chuckled. "She had wonderful things to say about you too."

She giggled.

"Is there anything else you think you'll need before then? Any toiletries?"

"Toilet what?"

I smiled to myself. "Soap, shampoo, toothpaste, items like that?"

"Oh!" She laughed. "Bryant, if we plan to spend the weekend together, you'll need to bring your vocab down to my level a bit, you know?"

I snorted. "Your level is not below mine for me to bring it down."

She snickered. "*That's* a total lie."

I licked my lips. Her modesty was humbling for me.

"I still haven't figured out what you want from me. I'm sure I am nothing like the other women you've entertained."

"I want you to pose as my girlfriend for a night," I replied.

"Yeah, I get that. What I don't get is why me?"

"Why not you?" I retorted.

There was silence on the line before she released a gust of air. "I'm just not..."

"Not what?"

"Nevermind," she answered. "I'm going to get a little more rest. Today is my day off and tomorrow will be insane at the beauty salon I work at with New Year's Eve approaching."

"Oh, yes, of course." I sat up in my seat. "No problem at all. We'll be in touch the day before the 31st. I'll send a car to pick you up from your residence and my chauffeur will drive you to mine so we can arrive at the wedding together. Sounds good?"

"Sounds real organized." She snickered. "No wonder your name is on the brimming bank accounts. So authoritative. How can I say no to any of that when you've got it all figured out?"

I smiled once more, my cheek running smoothly against the mouthpiece of my cordless phone. "Speak with you in a few days, Zoe. Enjoy your rest."

"Bye Bryant."

I leaned my head back against the leather headrest of my chair and sighed like a middle-school child with a crush.

I scoffed a laugh at myself. "Bryant, stay focused."

EIGHT

"**G**ood morning, Mr. Townsend," I greeted steps away from him. "How are you feeling today?"

He glanced up at me and smiled. "Zoe! I'm well, beautiful."

Mr. Townsend was the neighborhood odd jobs guy. Actually, he was homeless and lived out of the shelter a mile south of here. Earned his money doing odd jobs around the neighborhood, like sweeping litter up from in front of bodegas or helping landlords during the winter by shoveling snow. When he wasn't doing that, he spent his time in front of the neighborhood laundromat, parked on a tiny black milk carton crate, opening doors in exchange for a little change.

"I got you this chicken parmesan sandwich from the sandwich shop down the block." I handed it to him. "Figured, you could use a little lunch for the day."

I always tried to help out wherever I could. He never liked just asking for money. Only preferred to get it by doing something legit for it. So, whenever I was around, I bought him lunch.

His face lit up. "You're always looking out for an old man, Zoe, I swear." Mr. Townsend made quick work of the parchment paper around the sandwich. "It smells great, thank you."

I smiled. "You're very welcome. Now, you take care, all right?"

"I'll try."

I approached the laundromat door and Mr. Townsend hopped up off his crate to grab the door for me.

I placed my bag filled with detergent and fabric softener on the floor to dip my hand into my jeans' pocket and handed him a ten-dollar bill. He shook his head and his hand.

"Now you know this is too much," he chastised.

"Mr. Townsend, no, it is not." I pushed the money in his hand and gestured with my chin at the crate outside holding his sandwich. "And don't waste your time arguing with me about it. Your sandwich will get cold if you do."

He laughed.

I lumbered through the door of the laundromat with the slack of my laundry bag resting on my shoulder blade. In my other hand, I clutched the bag filled with my detergent, fabric softener bottle, and a box of dryer sheets.

The place was empty for a Sunday. It seemed everyone was procrastinating until during the week to take care of their chores. I wouldn't have time for that since I would be in Long Island by Tuesday.

"Hey Zoe," I heard ahead of me.

"Hey T!" I approached her and stepped between her outstretched arms. "What's up, girl?"

I'd known Tonya since high school. Like me, she never left the hood. Stayed behind, worked, had two kids, and was just getting by.

She sighed while shaking her head. Her jumbo box braids fell to her shoulders as she balanced herself on the arches of her feet to add fabric softener to her machine. "Girl..."

"What?" I dropped my bag of clothes and laundry stuff to the floor and pulled open the washing machine door beside her.

"Can you believe my landlord, Mr. Calvin, is putting all of our asses out?"

My brows shot up.

"*Mm-hmm.* Giving me and the other tenants until the end of January to find new places. He's not accepting rent for February. So regardless if we secure a spot or not, we got to go."

"Shut up, why?"

"The nigga sold the building!"

I paused adding my clothes to the machine to stand upright and face her. "He did what? That building has been here from before I was even born."

"Supposedly, they want to change the units into condos or something like that. I think they're planning to knock the thing down and to rebuild like they've been doing with the other buildings in the area."

I kissed my teeth while hunching forward to add the last of my clothes to the washer. "That is so fucked up. I'm so sorry, T."

She shook her head. "Now, I got to find another place for me and my kids. The landlord fixed the rent over there. Now, I'm gonna be paying double that shit unless I just move down south like everybody else is doing."

"Hmph," I huffed. "The south is too hot for me and the pay is lower than up here because the cost of living is less."

"I know, but what choice I got, Zoe?"

"I know."

Brownsville had been changing at a fast rate. One day there's a chicken spot, the next it's a coffee shop. The change had been gradual but more and more, I've been noticing different faces around the area, more than usual.

I was dropping coins into my machine to start it up when I asked Tonya, "Have you checked out some buildings around here?"

"Girl, they're asking for almost 2K for a two bedroom," she answered. "I'm gonna need another job on top of my two just to cover rent and utilities. Don't even get me started on having enough for food to put in my fridge. I keep trying to get benefits, but they keep telling my ass I make too much. Too much to get help, but not enough to provide on my own. And their father is a whole other issue with his broke, selfish ass. I'm just over this shit, Zee, seriously."

I sighed, feeling defeated. Seeing my girl like this hurt my heart.

"Well, listen." I moved in close. "If you need anything, you can come to me, T. If you need extra cash, someone to watch the kids while you work, anything, just tell me ma, and I got you, aight?"

She smiled with all her teeth then pulled me in a hug, wrapping her arms tight around me. "Thanks Zee."

She stepped out of her embrace. "I'll keep that in mind, but I like to provide on my own."

"I know." I tilted my head. "Just don't be too proud to ask for help. I'm always happy to."

She bobbled her head up and down. "I'll try to remember that."

While adding soap to the machine, she asked, "What you doin' for New Year's Eve?"

"I got a wedding I'm going to."

"Oh, that's dope! A New Year's Eve wedding? Yeah, that sounds official. Who you going with?"

"Some guy," I replied, not at all wanting to reveal who. I wasn't familiar with Bryant's public persona, but I'm sure Tonya was and I wasn't up for the questions or lying to her.

"Well, anybody other than that loser Rocco is an upgrade. He really out here running around with Kali like it's cute."

"Girl, they deserve each other. Let them self-destruct together."

Tonya cackled.

"He found himself in front of my building begging for me to take him back then in the same breath saying I won't do better than him."

"He can eat a dick with that."

I laughed out loud.

"I'm sure this new guy is about to show you some things you ain't never seen. It be like that when you end a dead ass relationship. God be waitin' to bless you. Giving you better when your heart is as pure as yours, Zee."

"You know what, T?" I turned to face her with a huge smile on my face. "I hope you're right. 'Cause Lord knows I can't deal with another lying ass man."

———

A few miles from the exit ramp we rolled off of, we pulled up to a gated entrance with the initials *B.G.* front and center on the wrought iron frame. By *we*, I meant myself and the chauffeur Bryant sent to my apartment building to pick me up. The brother was the nicest driver I'd ever met. He even left his car and hiked up the five flights of stairs to grab my luggage, and the garment bag with my dress, and lugged both down to place in the car for me.

"Wow," I whispered to myself as I leaned forward in my seat to get a better view of what laid before my eyes. In the distance, I saw the blur of an enormous property. The place appeared to take up a huge chunk of land. It also looked like it was built in layers, like a cake. Near the back of the property curved outward, forming a large circular dome roof that rounded and disappeared toward the back of the mansion. I couldn't be too sure, what with all the trees surrounding it.

"Hey Donovan," a man dressed in all black greeted outside the vehicle at the gate. His coat was unbuttoned, so I spotted the gun secured in its holster at his waist. "You can head right in," the guy told the driver.

As the car continued up the path, the house came more into view. A house was an understatement because this resembled a castle the closer we drove.

"He lives in this?" I asked the driver.

He chuckled. "He sure does. Beautiful, isn't it?"

"This joint is bad... *bad* as in good."

His chuckles grew into a laugh and I giggled at myself too.

My eyes fell on the expanse of grassy lawn and manicured hedges first. Directly opposite the house was a big water fountain that sat in the center of the winding road. The windows were grand. I'd never seen windows this high in my entire life. To the left of us were luxury cars, a few of them parked in front of what I determined to be a multi-car garage.

The moment the car stopped in the middle of the winding driveway, the front door of the property opened, and out walked Bryant. Well, he swaggered actually. Taking poetic strides toward the car dressed in just a pair of slacks, leather boots, and a black wool sweater.

The moment he opened the door he said, "Welcome, Zoe."

Bryant extended his hand toward me to take, and I held on as I stepped out of the car.

My eyes were everywhere. On the large-paned windows, on the

majestic structure of the property from the outside. It was like I stumbled onto a movie studio set. Everything was so grand.

"Donovan," Bryant stated above me. "Leave your car here and head inside. I had Victor whip up a quick lunch for everyone. Help yourself to something."

"Thanks, Mr. Greene." Donovan tipped his hat. "Will do."

"Shall we," I heard closer to my ear. When I gazed up in his direction, all I could do was nod.

I thought the outside was jaw-dropping. The moment I got inside, my eyes almost popped out of my skull.

We stepped through the double front doors that opened to a large entry way. The ceilings were as high as the ceilings in an indoor mall. Crown molding everywhere, two curving staircases I was sure led up to bedrooms or heaven. And the chandelier, my God, the chandelier was as big as one of those luxury vehicles parked out there. My eyes rolled down to below my feet to see the floors covered in expensive ass white marble with black veins.

"Are you hungry?" Bryant asked behind me.

I twisted my neck, then my body to face him.

"I wasn't sure of what you preferred to eat. You said you eat everything, but that wasn't specific enough, so I made a request that my chef prepare a few things that should suit your palette."

"Are you real?"

A beautiful smile spread across his lips and I had to take a breath to keep standing.

"First." I spun around to get a full view of the front area. "Let's get clear on something. *This* is *not* a house."

He studied me, his brows gathered in confusion over his eyes.

"You said you could have a driver pick me up from my apartment and to drive me here to your house. *This* is not a damn house, Bryant. It's a palace."

His laugh reverberated around us. "I didn't want to overwhelm you by saying *my mansion*. That sounds so pompous to me."

I stared up at the sparkling chandelier, feeling like I needed sunglasses to take it all in. "It's honest. But even calling this a mansion is an understatement."

"Would you like a quick tour before we head out?"

I whipped my head in his direction. "Um, yeah!"

And a tour is what I got.

Outside of the property satisfied my wildest dreams, but inside floored me. Bryant took me around his mansion, directing me first to the living room. My eyes soaked in the visuals of upholstered furniture made with oak wood finishings and art work that made absolutely no sense to me but were beautiful and worked with the living room's decor. We visited the kitchen that was bigger than my entire apartment's floor plan. Before heading up those winding stairs, we turned the corner from where we entered the mansion and I gasped. Down the long walkway he led me. Against the walls and curved overhead was an indoor aquarium. An assortment of fish swam to the left, the right, and above me. I tilted my head back to take in the coral and tank essentials.

"This is *so* beautiful, Bryant," I whispered to myself. "My God."

Bryant turned to glance at me over his shoulder, still leading the way. "It's my third favorite place in the property."

After seeing his home office, the home library, and his enormous wine cellar that was the size of a SoHo boutique, we stepped onto the elevator on the ground floor and took it up to the second floor. The mansion had ten bedrooms. Ten amazingly decorated bedrooms outfitted better than any hotel I've stayed in. Each room had textured wall accents and fireplaces. But the best room was his.

Angel's might as well had harmonized a tune when he pushed open the double doors to his master bedroom suite. Automatically my eyes went to his windows straight ahead framed by heavy gold curtains. The view opened to the water. All I could see was partly cloudy sky and ripples of water.

"Bryant," I said to him. "You've got to be kidding me right now."

I made my way to his floor-to-ceiling windows and sighed at the view. It was the most calming thing I'd ever seen, and all that was there was water.

"My second favorite part of the house," he announced behind me.

When I turned to him, my eyes moved around his room instead. Taking in the round king-sized bed with a TV at the foot of it. More paintings and artwork decorated the walls. Custom lighting hung over the center of the room. And his walk-in closet was the size of a studio apartment.

This was all too much and so humbling at the same time.

"Let me show you my favorite part of the property." He gestured with his head toward his bedroom's door.

"Oh, there's more?" I joked. "This place gets better?"

All he did was laugh as he led the way.

We were back on the elevator and heading down to the lower level of the property. On this level, the man had an in-home theater complete with his version of a concession stand filled with popcorn, candy and chocolates. But that couldn't compare to the room he escorted me to that immediately made my eyes cloud with tears.

We stepped into a dark theater, a huge dome with a ceiling that curved into a gigantic circle overhead. I instantly recalled this part of the mansion sticking out from outside and it being a mystery to me when I arrived on the property. Inside, the lights were low, damn near off, and the theater had seats that angled up to form a semi-circle. But up above, and against the ceiling, were the real attractions - stars and orbiting planets.

"This is my planetarium," he explained low beside me. "I come here often to de-stress and to think."

My eyes followed the shooting star dashing across the ceiling and disappearing into the darkness behind us.

I couldn't speak. For the first time in a long time, my surroundings rendered me speechless.

"I see you like it," he said.

All I could do was nod, my eyes still trained above me.

I exhaled a gust of air through my mouth and looked over at him. We stood only a few feet apart, but I swore I could hear his heart beating. Without even realizing it, a tear fell from my eye and then another. Before I could stop myself, I was crying silently. Without hesitation, Bryant reached over to wipe my tears away and offered a warm smile.

"This place has that kind of effect on people, I've learned." He tilted his head back to study the space above again as if he were seeing it all for the first time and added, "You never realize how small you are until you stare into outer space. This room is humbling to me. It's where I come to feel tiny when my head gets too big."

I nodded once more.

"When I come in here, I can't help but to feel like no matter how big of a problem I'm dealing with, it isn't bigger than anything outside of me, which makes it doable or something I can handle."

"Yeah," I agreed. "The energy in here is something I've never experienced before. This room is charged. Almost intoxicating."

"Speaking of intoxicating. Let's grab something to eat and drink then head out... mostly drink." He extended his hand out in front of him.

"Yeah, I need a little something to calm these nerves."

"My grandmother has called me twice in one hour just to confirm that you will be in attendance at my cousin's wedding."

I giggled, making my way out. "Okay, so let's not keep her waiting."

NINE

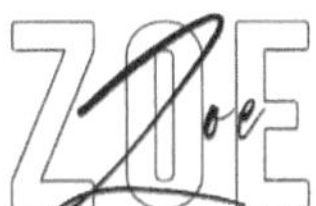

As soon as we arrived at *Gold Coast Castle*, the venue where the wedding would take place, it was like stepping onto another movie set. The place was amazing. Saying it was only amazing seemed lazy because it was so much more than that. In less than two hours, I'd visited two different large estates and the energy of everything was beginning to rub off on me. Or was it the alcohol?

Before leaving the mansion, Bryant and I had gone tit for tat on a gold label bottle of champagne, me probably more than him. I needed to find my calm. Socializing wasn't ever an issue, but this kind of mingling was next level. We were pretending to be a couple, for goodness' sake. But honestly, although I've never cared for this life or what it came with... I had to say I liked this; I liked it a lot.

The wedding planner pulled Bryant away the moment we stepped out of the car. He explained to me during the drive here that he'd contributed to the cost of the event and needed to sign off on a few things before the ceremony.

In one room in the castle is where I got dressed. My head was light, but somehow I wiggled into my outfit without losing my balance. My gown was something simple. Black, of course, long-sleeved, fitted and velvet. There was a long split that extended from the hem to near the top of my thigh. I thought it would be a bit much for a wedding, but Teagan insisted the gown was perfect for my physique and promised I would wear it beautifully. I still had my doubts, so I took a few photos of myself in the mirror at the boutique and texted the selfies to my girl Joi. She replied with, *yesssss bestie, this is the one! You look like a billionaire's wife! Own it.* I laughed while shaking my head. She was always so extra, but I knew then by her response that the dress was perfect.

After applying my makeup, gathering my locs to the top of my head, and securing the locs in a bun as best as I could in my state, I snapped a photo in the mirror and sent it to Teagan next, as promised.

"Wow," I heard behind me.

I turned to the voice to see Bryant standing there dressed like a whole fucking snack and sporting glassy eyes.

The man was fine on any other day, but that evening, the last evening of the year, as the sun set for the last time in 2019, he appeared breathtaking.

"Wow at you," I said back. "You look great."

"And you look..." His voice trailed off as he blew air through his lips, eyes tracing the curves of my body.

He wore all black, even down to the velvet black tie. Tailored fitted slacks and jacket, with a button-down shirt that thankfully failed to keep his pecs contained. Bryant was a sight to take in all at once. My eyes circled back to the velvet black tie.

"Where'd you get dressed?" I asked. "I didn't hear you come in."

"In another room," he replied, eyes still preoccupied with everything besides my eyes.

I gestured at his tie. "So that's why Teagan insisted on my velvet dress."

"I must send her an extra check because she has outdone herself." His eyes were so busy coasting up and down my frame, he'd forgotten to make eye contact.

"Um, Mr. Greene?" I teased. "Should we head down? The ceremony should be starting any minute now."

He shook his head as if it helped to ground him, and I giggled.

Finally his eyes met mine, and my heartbeat banged harder.

God, he's gorgeous.

He nodded first. Then when he found the words he told me, "Yeah, let's go."

I strutted my way up to him, his eyes down at my hips again. Though the champagne continued to course through my veins, I still balanced myself in my six-inch heels. Even with the six-inch boost, Bryant still had me by several feet.

"I have to be honest with you though." I smoothed my hand down my dress. "I think I just crossed over from tipsy to two breaths away from drunk."

He chuckled. "I think I'm close behind."

"So please," I added. "Don't hold me accountable for too much tonight."

He licked his lips slowly and pulled opened our door to step out.

The grounds were scenic. Everything so fairytale like. Large pale pink blooms of flowers covered everywhere there was a surface on the property. Shiny crystal sparkled from the ceilings to the pearl-like floors and from every angle. But the showstoppers were the waterfall of golden lights that hung off the edges of tree branches outside and the ceilings inside, lighting up the night. The evening of New Year's Eve was one of the coldest that year, but the wedding was hosted inside. Even in the driest of weathers, even when outside of the property where all the manicured hedges were barren of leaves and the grass laid less than green, there was still something about it that was gorgeous.

"During the summer," I heard a woman's voice say behind me. "Everything is absolutely stunning!"

I turned to find Bryant's grandmother, dressed in a stunning floor-length black gown, and a matching fur shawl draped over her shoulders.

"Mrs. Bryant." I approached with outstretched arms. "You look gorgeous."

She wrapped her arms tight around me.

"The best hugs, I swear it," she squealed before taking me by the shoulders and holding me out at a distance. "And you! Like a black Jessica Rabbit, my goodness. Absolutely stunning!" She leaned in. "I know women who would wipe their children's trust funds clean for your natural curves. Good for you!"

I laughed, and she joined me.

"I see my grandmother has found you," Bryant commented as he approached, two glasses of champagne in each hand.

"*More*?" I mouthed, shocked.

He shrugged, handing me my glass.

"Oh, but of course!" Mrs. Bryant replied. "You two belong on a magazine cover somewhere. Love the matching touch of the bow tie and the dress. I've taught you well, my loving grandson."

I giggled to myself, angling the rim of my champagne flute to my lips, then gazing up at Bryant to see him lowering his view to me.

Throughout the night, I caught him doing that a lot. Watching me, peeking at me from the sides of his eyes.

By this time, I was definitely drunk, but I prided myself on holding my liquor well. I was the cheerful kind of drunk, flirty, as my girl Joi would say.

Just keep your pussy in your dress, Zoe, I thought to myself.

As the pastor spoke during the ceremony, and Bryant's cousin and her new husband exchanged vows in front of us, Bryant's eyes kept moving to me.

"I'm *not* the wedding," I whispered to him while pointing ahead of us. "Focus that way."

"It's hard to ignore the fact that you are as stunning as the event though, Zoe. Can you really blame me?"

I smiled to myself, biting my bottom lip. Mr. Greene was certainly drunk too. I questioned if sharing that bottle of champagne before we left his mansion was a good idea.

I pinched the corners of my eyes as my body swayed on its own.

"Are you all right?" he asked.

"Yeah," I answered. "I just feel really *nice*."

He chuckled low.

The reception wasn't as subdued as the ceremony. In fact, things were about to take an interesting turn.

After the first dance and speeches, Bryant's cousin, Addison, stood up beside her new husband at their sweetheart table, tapping the side of her champagne glass with her fork.

She placed both down to lift her microphone and said, "Jason and I are so happy to share this night with the people we love so much. We want to extend our gratitude to everyone for attending tonight. To my amazing cousin Bryant, over there..."

She pointed in our direction and Bryant lifted his glass of champagne in response.

"Your contributions without us asking have made our day even more special. Thank you *so* much." She kissed her hand and stretched her arm in Bryant's direction. He offered a warm smile in return.

"Since I'm a hopeless romantic, as you all can see by all the fairytale-like fixings at this wedding..."

Everyone laughed.

"I want all the couples tonight to join in on the love that Jason and I have for one another."

I arched a brow.

"Every time Jason or I tap our glasses, we want for all the couples in the room to share a kiss. Fill this room with so much affection that we can swim in it. Let's see who will make this room overflow with love the most. Game on love birds!"

I'd had my share of champagne, true, but I knew I couldn't have misheard her.

"Oop," I droned to myself, lifting my glass and finishing what I had left in it.

"Oh!" Bryant's grandmother twisted in her chair to face Bryant and I. She clapped her hands and smiled from ear-to-ear. "I've taught that granddaughter of mine well, too, eh?"

I turned to glance at Bryant at the same time he turned to face me. He leaned in close and explained, "We don't have to join in if you don't want to."

The sweet scent of champagne on his breath made my nipples pebble and tingle in my dress. I dropped my view to his soft, full lips and sighed in defeat.

Fuck.

I learned that night that a lot of champagne not only made me happy and flirty. It also made me horny. I examined those lips of his, plump and full, glossed just right to entice. I clutched my thighs beneath the table the longer I stared. Intoxication also had me feeling like I'd be a fool not to seize the day. Only someone foolish would turn down kissing a billionaire. I'm not the superficial type in any sense of the word, but even I knew that.

It's crazy what liquid courage can provide to you when you're caught in the moment though, because without hesitation, I parted my lips and told him, "What makes you think I wouldn't want to."

His brows shot up and a devilish smirk played on his lips.

In what seemed like slow motion, the clinking of glasses at the sweetheart table made my breath hitch. Bryant's eyes softened in front of me as he placed his glass down on the table in front of him without paying a second glance and reached a hand to the side of my face. The moment he leaned in close, my eyes collapsed closed.

This. Was. Happening. And in real time...

His lips were warm on contact, so welcoming I couldn't stop the moan from humming behind my closed mouth. Without a plan, I parted my lips and so did he. Our tongues touched, and it sent an electric charge through my body. The clinking of the glasses, the applause in the background, everything muted. Behind my shut lids and in my mind, Bryant and I were alone. On his tongue, I tasted remnants of mint mixed in with the champagne he drank moments ago. His free hand moved below the table, his forearm coiling around my waist, moving me and my chair closer as he took our kiss deeper. And I let him, trusted him enough to make the journey a satisfying one. He groaned in my mouth and the walls inside me pulsed. A trip to the bathroom for me would be necessary after this because I could sense my primal response to his man-moan from the warmth of the seat below me.

By the time we broke our kiss and leaned away from each other, our lids were low and it seemed to be a shortage of air in the room.

Everyone surrounding us erupted in applause. We were far from the only couple there, but that didn't keep everyone's eyes from being glued to us. I only noticed this after peeling my eyes off Bryant, who I'm sure kept his eyes on me.

"Damn cousin!" Addison shouted into the mic from her chair at the sweetheart table while fanning herself. "You and Zoe win. That was so hot!"

I sat back in my seat and grabbed my glass, choosing the water this time, finally actually, in hopes it would cool me off. When I turned to Bryant, I caught him taking stock of me with hunger in his eyes. I'd never seen that look in his eyes before tonight. It made me glance away shyly.

In my ear, he whispered, "Wow."

I blushed.

"Was that just for show?"

"I'm good, but I'm not that good of a pretender, Bryant," I said back, finishing my water.

He smiled at me while leaning away, lifting his glass of champagne to his lips to finish what remained.

The wedding was a success. A night of dancing, socializing, making up more stories concerning Bryant and my relationship and how our courtship started. By the end of the night, everyone was so loose, there wasn't a sober guest in attendance, not even Bryant's grandmother, Mrs. Bryant.

They had no idea who I was, but they all treated me like a princess, something totally new to me. Being here and with him was like living a dream, a fantasy. People treated me differently, in a good way, while I was on Bryant's arm while dressed like I was headed to the Oscars. A part of me didn't want for the night to end.

That champagne might as well had been bottles of vodka, the way my body soaked it up and made my head even lighter. I promise I was floating, with no clue how I could still remain on my feet. I'd never thought myself to be such a lush. Then again, I'd never drank the way I drank that night. It was more me being nervous than being interested in the champagne, although it really tasted better than the cheap stuff I got from the liquor store around my way on every other New Year's Eve. Tonight, I had way above my limit and obviously, Bryant had too.

After the wedding ended, Bryant and I rode the elevator to our room in the castle. He leaned one shoulder against the elevator's wall to face me. That man inspected me silently from my head to my six-inch heels, heating me up the longer he stared.

"You really are beautiful tonight," he told me. "You're beautiful every time I see you, but tonight your beauty is distracting me in a good way. A great way."

"You're drunk," I whispered, my head turning away. "*Very* drunk."

"I'm tipsy," he corrected.

"No, we were tipsy at the mansion. This right now? Is drunk."

He licked his lips. "And why is that worth mentioning?"

"We're not thinking straight."

"I apologize if I haven't made this clear to you from my kiss." He closed the space between us. "Being forward is something I tend to be more of in business, so I may have been a little lax with you. Please let me fix that. Zoe..." He stepped in front of me, pressed his hands to the elevator's wall on either sides of me, caging me in. "I don't want to think with you, and certainly not right now. I *think* for a living, far too much I might add, and right now I'm off the clock and wish to remain there for once."

I stared up at him for a moment then asked, "So if... umm." I cleared my throat. "If you don't want to think, *what* do you want to do?"

He left my question unanswered and leaned in, pressing his lips to mine again before I stepped back and out of the kiss. My shoulders were flush against the elevator's wall when I laid my hand against his chest meeting my eyes with his once more. He took my hand - that laid on his chest - in his soft grip and lifted it to his lips to kiss. Bryant used that same hand to pull me close a second time, to crush his lips against mine again. He slid me his tongue this time, and I accepted without pause, moaning on his lips. My temperature climbed three degrees above normal.

He smoothed his hands down the soft velvet of my dress to palm my ass through the fabric.

Bryant growled on my lips and I swear my legs almost gave out beneath me.

The elevator doors glided opened, and he guided me out, still joined by the lips. Bryant pressed me to the opposite wall outside of the elevator car where he slid his hand through the slit of my dress in route to my thighs, lifting then hooking my leg around his waist.

He freed my mouth for a moment to trail kisses down my neck before sucking on the delicate skin above my collarbone.

I peeled my eyes opened to peek down both sides of the hallway. "Damn," I whispered while clinging to him when I felt light on my feet.

I shut my eyes and let myself indulge in the sensation of having his mouth on my neck. Tried my hardest to push away thoughts of someone finding us in the castle's halls, literally necking.

"Bryant," I whispered. "We have to get to our room."

"I'm not sure I can make it there."

Bryant's fingers left the outer edge of my thigh, smoothing between them in search of warmth.

I gasped, immediately locking eyes with him. He leaned my head back with his free hand, and I bit down on my lip in anticipation.

My moan reverberated down the hallway the second the tip of his finger brushed against the sensitive glans of my clit.

"Bryant—" Before I could finish my thought, he circled my tiny bulb with his fingertip with a slow move that made me squeeze my lids shut and tuck my lips in my mouth to shut up.

I was so wet, dripping, his finger strokes were audible between us.

My eyes opened to his to find his lids low, eyes burning with something different from any other time we'd encountered each other.

This felt like a dream. A very vivid and very wet dream.

With our gazes locked, Bryant targeted my clit. Didn't move his finger to any other part of me, just kept it there. Circling and stroking, circling and stroking, until I could think of nothing else besides conceding and meeting his well-timed strokes with my hips.

"Yes, that's it." He leaned in again, this time gripping my bottom lip with the bite of his teeth.

The move sent me over the edge. A coiling in my abs made me jerk forward twice. I clasped my hands to his shoulder blades, my eyes closed, and I gave my body permission to come right there in that hallway. He slowed his massage the moment I closed my eyes and slacked my jaw. I forced myself to tuck my lips back in my mouth to keep from making too much noise.

When I opened my eyes to his, he was staring right at me. He hid his bottom lip in his mouth before he dragged that lip between the bite of his teeth.

"That was beautiful," he intoned. "I'm making it a priority to make you do that again." Bryant took me by the hand and led me to our room.

I could barely walk there, my legs wobbly from what had happened moments before paired with being drunk as fuck.

I hoped I could remember everything that happened tonight so I could fantasize about it later.

The second we stepped over the threshold of our suite, Bryant turned me to face the wall beside the door and reached for the zipper of my dress.

It all seemed like a movie, what was happening. Just that morning, I was strolling up my Brooklyn block and now, here I was in a castle with a billionaire who was eager to fuck me... *me*!

Maybe this is a dream.

I dropped my head in front of me and squeezed my eyes closed again, thinking that would wake me up.

Bryant smoothed down the sides of my dress to remove it. I dragged my nails down the silk quilted wall and exhaled.

"If this is a dream," I stated out loud but low enough for only him to hear me. "Then this is the realist dream I think I've ever had in my life."

When he turned me to face him, his eyes took in his view of me.

He took a moment to marvel at what he saw. After two beats he broke the silence by uttering low, "You're a masterpiece."

I was stunned by his words.

I couldn't contain my breathing. It was ragged, fast, as his eyes swept me from my head to my toes.

While shopping for my dress, Teagan insisted we stop by a store called *Agent Provocateur*. The entire visit, my eyes ballooned at the price tags on lingerie I considered being nothing more than strips of fabric. The cheapest thing there were the panties, and those were one hundred a piece. We settled on a lace set in black that she promised he would like. I swore to her he would never see it, not at all considering where the night would lead us. Man, was I wrong.

A smile pulled at my lips as I thought of Teagan and my exchange.

Bryant stood there for a moment longer, peeling the sleeves of his tuxedo jacket down his stacked arms. "Are you okay with this?"

I nodded.

"I need to hear you say it, Zoe."

"I'm okay with it."

How could I not be? For whatever odd reason, I'd ended up in this situation and I would be a fool to get in my way. I could hear my girl Joi going off in my head if I didn't seize the moment.

As he approached, his bow tie slipping from his fingers and dropping to the floor beneath us, I stopped questioning *why* he wanted me and started thinking about *where* he'd want me instead.

His hands made contact first before he pressed his body to mine. His grip slid to the back of my neck, which he used to bring me forward and into yet another kiss.

When we shared our first kiss down in the castle's ballroom, there was a spark. A literal spark of electricity that zapped our lips. I thought it was a coincidence, the champagne maybe, but when it happened again, in the room, against the wall beside the door, I exhaled all the air I had in me.

Bryant lifted me into his arms and carried me to the gold canopy bed.

Even in the dark, I remembered how immaculate everything was in that room when I got dressed in it hours earlier. I'd never experienced this brand of luxury in my life. Honestly, never cared to, but I would be a liar if I claimed it didn't add to the vibe.

I watched as Bryant unbuttoned his shirt. On an incline, I sat up and grasped the button of his trousers. He reached down, gently stopping me. Bryant peered in my eyes and told me to, "Just lay there and be patient."

The moment my back hit the bed again, he lowered down the sleeves of his shirt. The lights around the castle outside offered some sheen to the room, and the peaks and valleys of his muscles caught all of it.

I was able to memorize his physique when he stopped undressing to run his hand down his face and chuckled.

"I didn't plan for this... at all." He pinched the bridge of his nose. "I would have had you sign paperwork before we got this far."

"Paperwork?" I questioned. "What kind of paperwork?!"

"Please tell me you're on the pill."

"I am..."

"Last tested?"

"Um..." I cupped my hand to my forehead. *Was this really happening?* "Two weeks ago. I went to the clinic after my boyfriend cheated on me. I just needed to be sure everything was still all right with me. We've used condoms, but sometimes we didn't—"

"Results?"

"Negative. Everything," I replied, rolling my eyes now a little annoyed. "Yourself?"

"I haven't had sex in a year. Last tested last month. Also negative."

He stared at me. Well, not *at* me, at my body. His eyes examined every part of me from head to toe as he twisted his lips from left to right. I assumed he was finally thinking, the thing he said he didn't want to do.

"Maybe we shouldn't do this," I insisted. "You know... if you're having doubts. Not using protection is... we barely know each other and we really haven't—"

Bryant hooking his fingers around the band of his trousers and pulling it down, removing his boxers along the way, caused me to lose my train of thought.

"I trust you," he affirmed lowly.

The brevity of his words, as truly humbling as they were, went in one ear and out the other. That's because I couldn't believe the size of what sprang out of his clothing. My jaw dropped.

All he did was grin.

I inclined up again, my eyes measuring the length of him, my head tilting to the left. The brother was more than blessed from the shaft to the head. Long and thick with a slight curve to the right. My mouth watered just staring at it.

I shook my head in disbelief and made eye contact with him again.

"See, this right here ain't even fair," I started. "You can't be fine, have the money, *and* a big dick too."

A laugh tumbled out of his mouth.

"What book did you step out of?"

"Zoe, stop it," he said, shaking his head and holding a smile on his lips. Bryant lowered himself atop me, pulling me closer.

"No, seriously," I ran my hands over the broadness of his shoulders and sighed from how his hard muscles flexed against my palms. "Whose dream are you from?"

"*Shh,*" he shushed in my ear. I spread my legs wider for him when the soft head of his dick settled against my slick opening.

I leaned my head against the pillow below my head, eyes squeezing shut as he slid in unhurriedly. He released a long groan as he entered, inch by inch, his more than generous girth stretching me to my satisfaction.

"What's wrong with you?" I whispered, more so to myself. "You can't be this flawless."

Bryant took me by the chin when he'd finally filled me to the hilt. I opened my eyes to his. My walls fluttered around the column of his shaft in response to what I saw.

He crushed his lips against mine and left them there, leaving my questions unanswered, instead snaking his waist back and forth, plummeting his erection in and out of me with a skill new to me.

His strokes were mindful.

Purposeful.

Advanced.

He moved with a goal in mind.

His tongue thrusts copied his rhythm below the sheets. And I matched his pace, angling my hips to push forward each time he stroked up, doing my best not to wreck the flow.

Bryant groaned each time I did that, which encouraged me to do it more and with even more precision. He took his time, not rushing at all, never pausing either or disconnecting when he changed positions and sat me on top. I oscillated my waist over him while leaning back and pressing my hands to the top of his muscular thighs behind me. My head dropped back as I pushed my breasts forward and slid my hips back and forth over him. His hands roamed up and down my torso, his palms far from calloused but still strong. Below, he worked with me using instinctual moves, pumping up ever so gently, still allowing me to take charge. The moans and heavy exhales that left his lips let me know he was enjoying me as much as I was enjoying him, and that heightened my desire to keep riding. He grabbed me by the waist and turned with me, rolling me onto my back, never disconnecting. Below him again, I bit down on my lip and kept my eyes on his. I sped up my whines then eased back, so I'd let his dick stay hard while bringing him closer to his nut.

"Stop that," he said seconds later. He lifted one of my legs and placed it on his shoulder, turning his head to kiss my calf.

"You don't like it?" I moaned out.

"I like it too much." He moved his arms to either side of me, caging me in as he leaned forward, lifting me up in an incline by the hips while lowering just enough to kiss me, even given the angle. On my lips he added, "But you're coming before me beautiful."

The elevation placed him right at my spot, a spot he tapped, and tapped repeatedly until I couldn't move my tongue against his anymore.

I broke our kiss to say, "Come with me."

"Come *for* me."

He sped up and I couldn't even moan or focus on anything outside of us and off that bed.

Each time he found my spot, I expelled a breath until I stopped exhaling all together.

Without warning, my body warmed from the soles of my feet. A sensation flowed through me and bottomed out between my legs.

"Are you there for me, Zoe," he whispered on my lips.

I whimpered and grabbed the folds of the sheets in my hands.

"*Mmm.* Yeah, you're there. Enjoy beautiful."

All it took were two more thrusts to still me. The moment I blinked my eyes, I experienced a sweet and sudden implosion. My body convulsed and Bryant held me still, pressing his forehead against mine, maintaining his flow as his body quaked with me.

It seemed to last forever, me coming, definitely more than just a few seconds. My knuckles ached by the time I came down from my high from holding the sheets in my grip. Bryant inhaled and exhaled harshly as he slowly let my leg slide off his shoulder and my lower back touched the bed again.

He slinked down beside me, the back of his head hitting his pillow, chest rising and falling from exhaustion.

"I can't believe we just did that," were my first words to him once I caught my breath.

"Neither can I," Bryant panted between breaths.

His hand was at my face a moment later. He ran his fingertips down my mouth, gripped my jaw, and turned my head to face him, bringing his lips to mine once more and drawing me into another kiss.

TEN

ONE MONTH LATER...

"**S**URPRISE!"

The room of people shouted at the top of their lungs as my good friend Lennox's eyes grew wider by the second.

Music blasted from the floor speakers as we all made our ways over to greet him.

"Happy Birthday, brother," I told him as I pulled him into a hug.

"Thank you, thank you." He embraced me back. "I can't believe this right now."

More people followed in tow, pulling him into hugs and air kisses, and I just stepped to the side, finding the makeshift bar to pour myself a drink.

I was at my friend Lennox Walker's surprise 33rd birthday party. When I'd received the call from his best friend, Rylee Daniels, informing me that she and their parents were throwing a surprise party for him, I cleared my schedule immediately. It's not every day I get to celebrate a good friend's birthday.

My phone buzzed in my pocket and when I retrieved it, I noticed the message from Zoe.

Zoe: Hi.

That simple greeting made me smile. It had been a month since my cousin's wedding. Also, a month since Zoe and my hookup. I ran my hand down my face as I tried not to remember it. My behavior, what I did? Completely out of character by all accounts. And her reaction the next morning didn't help.

"Oh my God," I heard her whisper beside me.

The second I opened my eyes, the sunlight from the risen sun beamed through the drawn open curtains and attacked my view. Something usually so beautiful to behold, the sunrise, felt like a shard of glass had pierced through my pupils.

"Oh. My. God," she repeated, jumping out of the bed.

I groaned as I sat up, my head spinning. Excessive drinking was never my thing. Can't remember the last time I did it, if ever.

"Where are my panties?" she asked out loud.

When I turned my head her way, I saw her moving around the room frantically.

"Zoe," I rasped.

She froze in her steps, delaying turning to face me.

"Zoe," I repeated.

When she finally focused my way, her eyes were wild, mascara smeared, lipstick everywhere except on her mouth. She had on the gown she wore the night before, the zipper undone. She held the top half of the gown against her breasts.

She parted her lips to say something, but nothing came out.

"Everything okay?" I inquired.

She closed her eyes and licked her lips. "What happened last night was not me."

I wrinkled my brows.

"I mean, it was me," she clarified, "it just isn't something I usually do. At all. And I don't want you thinking—"

"I'm not thinking about anything right now besides getting an aspirin." I clasped the innermost corners of my eyes with my index and thumb fingers.

Her reaction was a relief, actually. What we did the night before, at least for me, was reckless. The first, second, and third rounds were abso-

lutely reckless. You don't get to a billion hooking up with random women and without a condom, no less. Nothing about Zoe was random, though. But we had an arrangement, and sex was not a part of it. And if it were, I would have had her sign a non-disclosure agreement like I do the other acquaintances I've had these types of nights with in the past. She was different though, and last night was the exception. As reckless of a decision as it was for us to take things there, and in the way we did, I wouldn't have changed anything about my decision.

"Have a seat," I insisted, lifting up and stepping off the bed.

Her eyes grew as I passed her on my way to the en suite, naked.

"I'll order us up some coffee."

She followed me with her eyes into the bathroom until I closed the door behind me.

For the rest of that day, she didn't say much. We bid farewell to my grandmother later that morning after breakfast. And that was it.

That was a month ago. Between that time, personal phone calls weren't an option. Zoe seemed uncomfortable with our decision to be intimate that New Year's Eve night, and I didn't want to add to that discomfort by contacting her just because. So when we spoke in the month since, it's been to arrange for her to select the car she wanted, the one we agreed I would purchase to replace the one she crashed into me with. She'd finally decided on a 2019 silver Camry, a car I was vocally against, but she was driving it. Who was I to argue with her about it? I scheduled the car's delivery at my mansion for tomorrow in which I planned to reach out to her and to have my driver pick her up from her home and drive her to the mansion for her to pick up herself. I could've arranged for the car to be delivered to her address, but honestly? I needed an excuse to see her again. So imagine my surprise to see her text me one day before. Instantly, I believed it had to be because she had plans to visit my home the next day.

I hope she doesn't cancel.

"Sexting?" a familiar voice quizzed over my shoulder.

I turned my head that way to see Lennox standing a few feet behind me.

"Goose-necking?" I shot back.

He laughed, raising his fist to his mouth to cover. I chuckled at the sight.

My friend appeared like his old self. It was impossible to tell that he'd just had surgery last month. He stood before me healthy, vibrant...

"Happy," I said out loud. "You look happy."

He blew air out of his mouth. "I am, man. I am."

His eyes drifted off into the distance and I followed his line of vision to see it land on Rylee who was sitting amongst a group of women laughing.

I turned my focus back on him to see him all dreamy eyed with a smile plastered on his face.

"Whoa," I said to him. "What is this?"

He twisted his neck in my direction.

"*You* and Rylee..."

He bit his bottom lip and leaned inward. "I think so. I *hope* so."

I arched both brows. "Can't say I'm surprised."

Keri Hilson's "Slow Dance" started up, her vocals streaming from the speakers.

Lennox tapped me on the shoulder twice and told me, "I'll be right back."

I watched as he approached Rylee and the group of women, extending his hand for her to take. When she obliged, I couldn't help but to smile at the two of them.

Their relationship has always perplexed me. I remember when I first met Rylee, and Lennox introduced the two of us, I believed she was his girlfriend. Their connection just seemed too good for them not to be an item. But they were only friends, friends who eventually had a child together.

As I watched the two sway in each other's arms to the song playing, I realized "just friends" was no longer what they were to one another anymore.

My phone buzzed again with another text.

Zoe: What time should I be there tomorrow?

Me: 11 a.m. works for me. Does it work for you?

Zoe: It does.

Me: So I'll send my driver to you tomorrow morning around 10:00 a.m.?

Zoe: That works. Thank you.

I inhaled a breath and slid my phone back into my pocket. I raised my glass of brandy to my lips and sipped slowly, curious how Zoe and my interaction would be like the very next day. Couldn't ignore the fact I was also excited to see her again.

The night wound down appropriately. I stood outside at the threshold of Lennox and Rylee's brownstone by midnight. The property was massive, inside and out. A beautiful piece of real estate that fit my friend to a T.

Lennox stood opposite me. I was the last guest to leave, and he insisted on seeing me off. "You never told me how things worked out with you and sweetheart who you had play your girl for a night."

I peeked over my shoulder at my security, who were too close for comfort.

"Paul," I called, "you and the guys can wait for me in the car. I'll be there shortly."

Paul nodded as he threw up hand signals to inform my two other guards to step into their SUVs.

"Can't say I miss that." Lennox chucked his chin toward my security.

I slid my hands into my wool coat's pockets. "Comes with the territory."

"You sent them off because you about to get real, huh?" Lennox smirked.

"We slept together that night," I revealed.

Lennox's eyes ballooned. "She signed an NDA before the wedding?"

I shook my head.

Lennox stepped back. "Bryant Greene out here hooking up with women without having them sign their lives away first?"

"Come on." I waved my hand in the air. "Don't antagonize."

He laughed. "She must really be something special."

"Why do you say that?"

"To have you step out of your comfort zone. First with having her car towed after she slammed into you, then with you asking her to act like your girlfriend, then sex without a non-disclosure agreement? Something you insist the women you entertain sign every time, no exceptions?"

I ran my hand down my face slow. "We had sex drunk."

He sandwiched his hands together and pressed his hands to his lips. "I'm sorry, who are you? Say that again?"

I chuckled. "We both had a lot of champagne first at my mansion, then at my cousin's wedding. By nightfall... things just got a little wild between us."

"Drunk behavior is just sober feelings." A smirk played on his lips. "Believe me on that."

"Hmph," I huffed. "I'll see her tomorrow."

He wiggled his brows. "For another round?"

"No, no." I laughed. "She's picking up the car, I promised her."

"And now you're buying her a car?" He laughed. "Yeah, you got it bad."

"I'm out of here." I extended my hand, which Lennox accepted.

"We gotta do lunch or dinner, something sometime soon B," he told me through his laugh.

"Next week," I confirmed. "My calendar is clear all week."

"Cool."

A second later, I saw Rylee descend the staircase over Lennox's shoulder. Lennox peeked that way, then turned to me again with a little sparkle in his eyes.

I chuckled. "Have fun."

"Oh, I intend to," he affirmed, extending his hand for another handshake.

"Next week," I decreed as I turned to step down their brownstone stairs.

"No doubt," Lennox called behind me. "We'll talk before then, though."

"Absolutely, take care."

"Later," he said to my back before closing the door.

———

"Zoe," I said when I turned the corner to approach the entry way of my mansion.

I'd been in my office since that morning. I usually worked from my office in the city, but after returning home from Lennox's party later than usual, I figured I wouldn't trouble myself with driving out to the city when I could conduct business from my home. Plus, Zoe was stopping by that morning to pick up her car.

She turned to face me, her locs loose and hanging down her shoulders and back. That day she wore a long puffer coat, beneath it a long camel-colored cable-knit sweater that draped over a v-neck tee tucked into formfitting matching joggers.

I tried not to have my mind return to that night, but seeing her for the first time since my cousin's wedding made that impossible.

"Hey," she greeted, closing her eyes when the smile she attempted to contain burst through.

She hid her lips in her mouth and turned away. Zoe pointed behind her to my closed front door. "Is that the car out there right now?"

"Yup," I answered.

"It's beautiful!"

"You're beautiful," is what I wanted to say, but I was sure it would make the moment awkward. So instead, I just nodded in agreement.

I gestured toward the door with my hand. "Why don't we go and—"

The chime of my mobile device in my pocket interrupted my offer. I pulled the phone out of my pocket and took a quick glance to see it was Rylee calling.

"Let's step out so you can check out your new car," I said to Zoe as I answered the call. "Good Morning, Rylee."

"Hey Bryant."

The sound in her voice stopped me cold. For someone who'd successfully pulled off what seemed to be a surprise party where Lennox enjoyed himself, the way she sounded made little sense.

Still I said, "You either partied too hard last night or you're coming down with something."

She exhaled a shaky breath into the phone.

"Oh wow!" Zoe commented ahead of me as she moved around her new car. "It looks even more amazing off the lot!"

"I... umm," Rylee mumbled, drawing my attention back on her. "I don't know how to say this. As many times as I've said it to myself, it has gotten none easier."

"Said *what* to yourself? What's going on?"

"You're one of the few people I'm calling about this, this soon, because you and Lennox are really close—"

"Rylee," I called with more bass. "*What* is going on?"

"Lennox passed away this morning."

Her words echoed in the corners of my mind. I'd stepped out of my home without a coat, but the cold that chilled my bones came from within.

I scoffed a laugh, sure I had to have misheard her.

"I'm sorry, Rylee," I started. "I think I... I don't think I heard you correctly."

She sniveled on the other end of my phone. "You... did."

"Bryant?" Zoe said a few feet in front of me. "You're shaking."

"How?" I asked into the phone. "I was just talking to him in person *last night*. Literally hours ago." My hand was at my brows as I stroked the hairs with my cold fingertips. "We're meeting up next week."

Rylee broke down on the line. Her wails and trembling cries made me drop my phone to the paved driveway beneath me.

Zoe marched up to me and placed her hand to my chest, tilting her head to one side to examine me. She glanced down at my phone on the ground, crouched down to pick it up, then pressed the device to her ear.

"Hello?" she spoke into the phone. "Hi, this is Zoe, Bryant's friend, who is this?"

She was silent for a moment, the phone to her ear. I couldn't move or speak. I stood frozen, repeating and replaying Rylee's words.

Lennox passed away this morning.

Lennox passed away this morning.

"Oh Bryant, I'm so sorry," Zoe whispered.

I was numb all over. I felt the weight of Zoe's hand on me, but my mind couldn't process anything.

"Come on." She guided me toward the front door. "Let's go inside."

One foot after the other, I walked with her until warmth washed over me from my indoor heating.

She placed my phone down on the table by my front door.

"What do you want to do?" she asked. "Do you want to sit down?"

"I need a drink."

"Bryant," she said low, "it's eleven o'clock in the morning."

I inhaled a trembling breath and locked eyes with her. "I *need* a drink."

She stretched out her arm to stroke my back.

I turned away from her touch and advanced toward my office, hearing her footsteps trail close behind me.

We passed below my aquarium arch of tropical fish and I pushed opened my office door, headed straight for the bar.

All I could think about was Lennox and our last interaction with each other. If I knew it would have been our last, I would have stayed longer, talked about every and anything we could.

A knot formed in my throat that I tried my hardest to swallow back. In my grip was my brandy decanter, which I held over a crystal glass. Poured out just enough to toss back in a gulp.

I'd lifted the decanter again and paused, my eyes zeroing in on my hand that shook, the contents in the bottle vibrating because of it. A soft warm hand covered mine, as Zoe gently took the bottle out of my hand and poured a decent amount of the spirit into the glass. She placed the bottle down, took my hand, then took the glass and escorted me over to my leather office couch.

For a moment, neither one of us exchanged any words. I sat on the cushion and she'd pulled up a chair to sit across from me.

"I lost a friend too once," she finally said after several minutes of silence. "When I was younger."

I lifted my head then my eyes to focus on her.

"She was my best friend. We were teenagers, sixteen." She ran her hand up her arm and squeezed her forearm. "Her name was Raquel. She was *so* pretty and *so* funny." Zoe smiled.

"It was the summer, during one of our neighborhood block parties. She didn't even want to go out, but I begged her to. My foster mother had finally agreed to me hanging out an hour past curfew. I'd been begging for two weeks for her permission. So I wanted to take full advantage of the freedom that day." She swallowed hard. "Anyway,

Raquel and I stopped at one of the corner bodegas to get sunflower seeds. I didn't want to go to that particular one because everyone knew some dope boys, the drug dealers?" she asked, checking my understanding. "That's where they hung out and sold most of their stuff. But she insisted, so I went too. There was a commotion outside as we were paying at the register. The second we stepped out, there were three shots fired. They sounded so far away, so they didn't alarm me. I'd heard them so many times before, so they were as common as firecrackers to me. But then..."

I stared at her, watching as her eyes pooled with tears.

"Then I looked to my right and didn't see Raquel standing there. Glanced down and saw her laid out motionless on the concrete below me with her eyes still open. She'd caught one of those bullets right here." Zoe pointed at her right temple.

I exhaled all the air out of me.

"I was a wreck after that," she revealed. "Spent a lot of time sleeping and just being a mix of sad and mad." Zoe tossed a few of her locs over her shoulder. "And when I was awake, I spent the days trying to relive the moment, rearrange the order of events that would have had her in school with me that fall. Her brother was going through it too, but way worse because, you know, it was his little sister. So he and I grieved together and eventually started dating a few months later. We'd been in a relationship up until last month."

"Sorry to hear that," I said.

She met her eyes with mine. "And I'm sorry about what happened to your friend. Truly I am."

I sighed, dropping my head over the neck of my couch, realizing this was really happening.

"You never get over it," she added. "At first, you'll think about it constantly. Other times when you have moments of joy, you'll remember what happened and will feel guilty for experiencing that joy while your friend can't anymore. But eventually you learn to cope, you reminisce about the good times. The loss will hurt out of nowhere on most days though, but go with it and remember him at his best."

I finished the rest of my brandy. "I don't know what their plans are yet," I said. "But if they have a funeral, I'd really appreciate it if you'd accompany me."

She moved her eyes off mine and pointed them down on my carpet.

"Unless, you don't want to—"

"No, I'll go with you," she acquiesced. "I can be there for you."

As simple as those words may have sounded leaving her lips, they meant the world to me and were the only things keeping me together in that instance.

ELEVEN

3 white doves flew out of a large ivory cage, their wings flapping against the air as they took flight high above the procession. Everyone wore white, including the bishop presiding over the service, who draped himself in a pure white robe that blew in the winter wind.

The bare trees cast shadows over solemn faces, most of those faces wet from tears. Designer sunglasses shielded eyes from the sun. For a funeral, the day was beautiful, not a cloud in sight. At a distance, there were sporadic flashes. Like short bursts of lightening as reporters and photographers stood afar capturing the funeral of famed former basketball player Lennox Walker.

Last year, the closest I'd ever gotten to a celebrity was when I saw Spike Lee in front of *Juniors* in Brooklyn. He looked regular, like someone you could approach and strike up a conversation with. Now here I was, sitting next to a billionaire, surrounded by celebrities I've seen on my television set, basketball players I've seen photoed on billboards just down the block from my apartment building.

I turned to my right to glance at Bryant. He'd been quiet from the time I drove up to his mansion in my new car to meet with him before leaving to attend the funeral. He moved his balled lips from left to right.

Every so often he swallowed back his tears. I placed my hand atop his icy hands and squeezed tight. He shared a look with me and offered a simple nod before retreating into his own world again.

The service at the church in Brooklyn was beautiful. The several speeches from friends and family were heartbreaking, true, but still full of light, many of them reminiscing about Lennox and how great of a guy he was. I didn't know much about him besides him being a dope basketball player who suddenly retired when he was his most popular. But based on what everyone had to say about him, he really was someone worth knowing.

Now at the burial site, some of us seated on plastic foldout chairs while others stood around on foot, we all crowded around a large ivory white casket, draped with an array of white flowers. My eyes moved to the woman with the baby on her lap. Smooth dark brown skin and braids swooped to the right side of her shoulder. She wore sunglasses and a heavy coat while she rocked from side to side. The arm of an older woman laid coiled tight around her shoulder. The older woman every so often used that arm to pull the woman toward her, to whisper something in her ear.

As the pastor closed with his parting words, and the casket descended into the gaping plot, Bryant stood up from his seat abruptly. I reached my hand for him, which he gently broke free from. His security was quickly on his tail, trailing him as he took large strides to the black SUV we arrived in. I sighed and stood myself to follow.

We'd returned to the church for the repast. The church was a megadome type place that appeared huge on the outside and even bigger on the inside. They held the repast in the church's basement, which seemed more like a ballroom. The set up was elaborate. A sea of white tables filled the space, framed by gold chairs. White cloth covered each table with a wall-to-wall table positioned near the back that held the food. This group was a social one. People moved about the room, introducing themselves and offering their condolences to Lennox's family. Bryant had done the same, and I stood by him as he did.

"Rylee," Bryant greeted the woman with the beautiful braids.

She turned to face him and pressed her hand to her chest first before extending her arms to him for a hug.

Rylee was gorgeous. Taller than me, with bright brown eyes, deep dish dimples, and a smile that sparkled even given the occasion.

"Bryant, thank you so much for everything, seriously," she told him. "The floral arrangements..." She pressed her hand to her chest again. "You know Lennox would have said this was too much, right?"

Bryant chuckled.

"But they were so beautiful. They really added to the day." Her eyes moved to me. "Hi."

"Hi, Rylee," I greeted with a warm smile. I briefly made eyes with Bryant.

"Uh, Rylee," he started, "this is Zoe, my—"

"Zoe," she whispered. "Yes, we spoke that day." Rylee moved in even closer, wrapping her arms around me, giving me no choice but to embrace her back. Her hug was so warm and welcoming.

"It's nice to meet you." She stepped back. "I wish it was under different circumstances."

"Yes, of course," I replied. "I'm so sorry for your loss."

She inhaled through her mouth then exhaled the same way. "Thank you. No matter how many times I hear that today, it still is so difficult to come to terms with this being real."

I tucked my lips in my mouth, understanding entirely. After losing my best friend Raquel, it took longer to get out of routine. Like stopping by her apartment to hangout. Or getting the urge to dial up her number whenever I experienced something I wanted to share with her.

"Well, if you need anything Rylee, anything at all, please know I'm just one phone call away," Bryant promised.

She smiled, two dimples appearing on each cheek again. "Thank you so much, Bryant. I really appreciate that." Her eyes moved off us and around the room. "If y'all will excuse me, I have to be social." She dropped her head into her hands. "I can't wait for this day to be over, seriously."

My heart broke for her as she ambled off to greet a few other people nearby.

"They just had a baby," Bryant revealed beside me. "Lennox and Rylee."

I squinted my eyes at him. "Really? I thought they were just friends."

He chuckled solemnly. "They were friends, but not only that. They were becoming more. That's the vibe I got from Lennox the last time I saw him."

Bryant raised his hands to his face to grunt into his palms. "He just celebrated a birthday."

I placed a hand on his chest. His eyes locked with mine and he didn't move them until I broke eye contact. His gaze caused my walls to pull in and I felt embarrassed. This was the last place I should have that kind of reaction.

"Let's head out," he said above me.

"Are you sure?"

"Yeah, I've had enough." Bryant turned on the heels of his *Louboutin*, chucking his chin to his guards, signaling that it was time to go.

———

On the drive back to Bryant's mansion, he sat quietly beside me, his fingers stroking the hairs of his mustache and beard. His eyes remained trained outside of his window the entire time. I bit at my lips, twisting them from left to right, trying my hardest to figure out how to best console him. He seemed so closed off that day, understandably. But damn, he could interact a little.

We arrived at the front gates of the mansion, the letters *BG* splitting in two as the wrought-iron gates parted.

Half a mile up, the driver pulled onto the winding road, stopping in front of the doors of the mansion. Bryant got out, and I followed, thanking the driver who'd gotten out to get our door.

The second we entered the mansion, Bryant took large steps toward his office.

I sighed.

The mansion was brightly lit. At the tender hour of five o'clock, it was pitch black outside.

I stepped out of my silver heels, hooked the back of them over my two fingers and headed in the direction Bryant disappeared in.

I ambled beneath the arch of his aquarium, my eyes drifting up and my head tilting back as I watched in awe how the fish swam overhead. This place was legit magical.

When I got close to his slightly ajar door, I noticed the lights were on, beams of it lighting up the opening.

I pushed the door open to find him sitting behind his desk, his fingers back to stroking the hairs outlining his lips.

I stood at the threshold until he made eye contact with me. Bryant hadn't shed a tear and had spoken little that day. He was holding a lot inside and I had no idea how to handle it. I understood wholeheartedly what he was going through, having gone through it too. But I never kept that shit to myself. I had Rocco and often we'd unload on each other how we felt about his sister's death. Bryant needed to talk.

So I asked, "Do you want to talk? You should talk about this."

His eyes moved off mine as he allowed them to roam down my figure.

After he asked me a second time to accompany him to his friend Lennox's funeral, Bryant arranged for his stylist, Teagan, to gather a bunch of white dresses for me to skim through. I was grateful for that. Shopping was never my thing, so having outfits picked out for me, especially by someone who already knew my size, was a blessing.

The dress I wore was an all white tailored midi-wrap dress. It clung to me, everything clung to me. No matter what I wore, the fabric of an outfit always clung to my body unapologetically. I had breasts, hips, and an ass that was hard to miss. So it didn't surprise me that was what had Bryant's focus.

I shifted my eyes away and took a breath. My body did that thing again under his scan. Walls pulling in, nipples hardening. But I figured this wasn't the time for that. We couldn't. Not at a time like this because if we did, that would make twice we hooked up in less than ideal conditions.

With my eyes off Bryant, I moved them around his office, gliding them along the large wooden desk, past the floor-to-ceiling built-in water fountain, over the mounted flat screen TV and allowed my view to finally settle on his mini-bar set up.

I dropped my heels by the door and crossed the threshold, closing the door behind me.

"You want a drink?"

He said nothing in response.

"Yeah, you want a drink."

I closed the space between me and the mini-bar, my eyes surveying the crystal bottles.

"I know you like brandy," I said to more so myself. "It would be easier to tell which one is brandy if you had labels on these bottles." I chuckled to myself. Wrapping my hand around bottle after bottle, I lifted them and sniffed inside the necks only to determine they all smelled alike.

I turned and asked, "Which one of these is brandy?"

Still, nothing. He sat there, his eyes fixed on my ass, and I scoffed a laugh, shaking my head.

"Fine," I told him. "I'll just pour into this glass what *looks like* brandy and you'll just have to deal."

After filling a glass halfway, I walked it over to him. He stood from his seat and met me in front of his desk, gently taking the glass out of my hand and tossing the drink back. His cheeks puffed until he swallowed twice, emptying his mouth.

"Aren't you supposed to sip that stuff?"

He licked his lips slowly, and I swallowed hard.

Bryant made his way around me and to the bar, picked up a different bottle, also brown, poured himself another drink and tossed that one back too, placing the glass down when he finished.

He grabbed another bottle and did the same thing. I sighed.

I leaned my backside against the lip of his desk and folded my arms. "Please don't spend the evening drinking."

He turned his head to glance at me over his shoulder.

"Find something else to do instead. Another escape. A healthy one. Because what you got in your hand won't seem like a good idea by the morning."

He placed the bottle down again and turned to face me. Bryant stared at me for a few beats. Finally, he made his way over to me.

"You'll have a headache and it won't help the situation."

He kept closing the space and before I knew it we were only a few inches apart.

"Bryant."

His hands landed on either side of my hips and I gasped. He smoothed his palms over the curve of my hips, moving to the roundest part of my ass.

"Bryant," I whispered this time. "Look at me."

When he did, I noticed the sadness in his eyes. It was clear he hadn't been sleeping. The space around his pupils was reddening.

I placed both hands to either side of his cheeks. "What are you doing?"

He left my question unanswered, redirecting his eyes down to my hips again, fingers moving up my torso toward the knot that held my dress together.

I turned my head away. Breathing got harder to do as my heart hammered in my chest. The longer his hands moved about my body, the wetter I got below that dress.

"Should I stop?" he finally asked, pulling one side of the knot on my dress loose.

I closed my eyes and squeezed my lids shut.

"Do you want me to stop?" he asked, pausing.

I took a breath and shook my head. Of course I didn't want him to stop. Honestly, I wanted him. I wanted *this* since that morning. I've wanted the weight of him settled between my thighs since the morning after his cousin's wedding, if we're keeping it really real.

I'd arrived to the mansion on time earlier today, but he was late getting dressed. For someone who's always been prompt with time, I knew it was the heavy load of the day that slowed him down.

So I waited in the kitchen. His in-house chef made breakfast and insisted that I eat before heading out. While finishing up, Bryant stepped into the eating area and I did a double take. His tailored white suit laid against him like he was a department store mannequin. His shoulders were broad, the suit's jacket failing to hide his bulging biceps. He'd just gotten a fresh haircut that added to the man's appeal. Even with the wrinkle of sadness covering his face that morning, Bryant was irresistible. I had to snatch my eyes off of him to get myself together. My gawking embarrassed me.

Now in his office, standing directly in front of him, his question swirling in my head, I shook my head again, giving him my answer.

"Say it," he demanded. "I need for you to say it."

With eyes still closed, I said, "I don't want you to stop."

He pulled at the rope, my dress slowly coming undone.

"But we can't keep hooking up like this."

Bryant went for the next string inside of the dress that kept the other half of the dress together.

"Hooking up like what?" he asked.

My dress was fully open, exposing another black lace bra and panties set from *Agent Provocateur.*

"The first time we were drunk." I searched for eye contact, but he was so distracted by my 40DDs. "Now..."

He ran his thumbs over my covered nipples and my words became a moan.

"I don't know," I continued. "I don't know if these physical interactions between you and me are healthy."

His hand brushed down my shoulders, knocking the fabric of my dress down my arms. I allowed the fabric to slip past my forearms, then my hands until it pooled around my bare feet.

"Why me, Bryant?" I asked, staring him right in the eyes.

"Zoe, why *not* you?" he shot back, not missing a beat.

Bryant leaned to the left side of me and swiped his hands once along his desk, knocking books, papers, and his phone to the floor.

I gasped when I turned to see them all scattered about.

He grabbed me by the waist to lift me up and place me on his desk.

His fingers moved to unbutton his suit's jacket, peeling it down his arms then moving on to his neck tie next.

With each item of clothing he paid attention to, to remove, my pulse raced. By the time he stepped out his pants and pulled off the tank he wore underneath his shirt, I lost my breath when I glanced down at his hard dick tenting his silk boxers. That thing the first time we met the night of Bryant's cousin's wedding had me speaking in tongue.

With one hand, he reached behind me and unhooked my bra.

Bryant had spoken only but a few words to me, but he clearly wanted me.

"You dull, Zoe." Rocco's insult faded in to recollection. "Your conversations are wack, sweetheart. Probably because you had nobody to teach you how to provide anything besides wet pussy, being a foster kid and all."

I shook my head, trying to ground myself in the moment again.

"You said you're on the pill, right?"

I nodded.

His fingers hooked the sides of my panties as he slid them down my thighs, flinging them across the floor.

My jaw dropped when he dropped to his knees in front of me and slid me closer to his waiting lips. I was in shock when his tongue made contact. My hips jerked forward in response. It didn't take long for my shock to wear off and for me to lose myself in the moment. Bryant moaned in response to my moans, angled the tip of his tongue to circle my clit. I dropped my head back between my shoulders, forcing myself to take breaths. Bryant didn't hold back. Sucking, flicking, and flittering his tongue clockwise, never changing pace or focusing anywhere else. I had a man worth more than I've ever seen in my lifetime down on his knees beneath me, serving me all he had like he had something to prove. I lowered my view and our eyes connected. He watched me watch him, tightening his grip around my thighs and pulling me closer to the action. I placed my hand to the top of his head and rolled my hips against his lips when the wave of my orgasm signaled it was close. He flicked his tongue twice more, and I splayed my thighs wider, giving in to my climax that rocked me from the inside out.

Bryant was on his feet, licking his lips of me as he pulled his boxers down. His dick jutted forward. He held the length of himself in one hand and used the other to move me closer to him by my lower back.

As he sunk into me slowly, my head fell forward, watching as he played a disappearing act between my lower lips. My walls expanded to accommodate his girth and my jaw slacked the deeper he tunneled into me.

He dropped his head back between his shoulders and released a long growl as he filled me, only stopping when I couldn't take any more of him.

My mouth hung opened even more as he slid back out and did that all again.

"Oh!" I hollered when he did it a third time. My fingers clasped to the edges of his desk to hold me up.

In and out he pumped. My eyes were closed when I felt his lips press against mine. He beckoned my tongue with his and shared my taste with me. My flavor was spiked with brandy. I moaned even louder at that and as he used his free hand to bury his fingers into my locs, thrusting back and forth with well-timed strokes.

Bryant balanced his palms on the mahogany wood below me, keeping one of my legs up by the prop of his forearm as he sped up his pace. There were people in and around the property. His chef, maids, security. I did my best to keep it down, but the way he fucked me on his desk gave insight he had no intentions of helping me keep quiet.

He pulled out and slid me off the desk, spinning me around. Bryant grabbed both of my wrists and encouraged me to lean forward and over his desk. He slid in from the back, no hands. He cupped his hands over mine as I hung on to dear life, clasping my fingers on the opposite edge.

"Please tell me we're more than this," I whispered.

"We're more than this," he confirmed, without hesitation.

His face was in my hair as he inhaled and exhaled me, never breaking pace. I bit down on my bottom lip, mentally climbing to that place of no return as he delivered long deep strokes from the back. My legs trembled the deeper he went. I felt him everywhere.

"You're my escape," he acknowledged against me.

I was slick down there, so slick gelled sounds echoed around us as he pounded in and out.

"Nothing else matters outside of you right now, please know that," he panted against me.

My eyes rolled, walls fluttered, body shook. He said all the right things, was hitting all the right places, detonating something deep within me. My orgasm teetered on the edge so I put any doubts out of my mind and resolved to meet the sensation head first. I threw my ass back toward him, scratching my nails along the surface of his desk when he found my spot.

"Yes, Zoe," he growled, increasing the speed.

"Bryant," I whispered.

"I know," he whispered back, angling his pelvis, a simple move that would send me over. "Me too."

With each last thrust, I moaned, and he groaned, our bodies defying gravity at least in my mind as I floated beneath him. No sound could leave my lips, no limb could move. I was in a trance again under him, not at all interested in returning to earth. If this was my life from here on out, I accepted it with open arms and no further questions or reservations.

I deserved this, I deserved him, and in that instance I deserved to come just like this. My legs gave out, and he held me up, keeping pace and groaning his strokes. I tucked my lips in my mouth and let myself go, shaking uncontrollably on his erection, reaching for anything around me to hold on to but really grabbing for nothing at all.

His warm release slid down my thigh as he kept pumping in and out. And in the depths of me, another orgasm prepared to take me over once more. It was in that moment, when my lips parted to release a silent cry and my eyes began to roll, reality was the lie and my dreams were the truth.

Twelve

She rolled her hips over me, sliding back and forth against my lap, eyes closed, fingertips digging into my pecs for balance.

In a matter of hours, I'd fallen in love with watching Zoe during sex. She became one with the act, mentally drifting off to a place she trusted me to bring her to each time I slid between her wet walls.

We'd literally watched the sun come up. After we both got ours on my office desk, we dressed at my insistence and quickly made our ways to my elevator to ride it up to my bedroom to continue. Sleep wasn't an option after that.

Her breaths were heavy. Sweat beads rolled down the middle of her breasts that bounced like globes whenever her body jerked from the sensation she created riding me.

Her locs swayed from left to right as she moved, adding to the visuals. I closed my eyes, indulging in the sucking effect her walls did around my erection.

"I could stay like this with you forever," she whispered. I smiled, loving that she enjoyed this, enjoyed me as much as I enjoyed her.

Her body jerked once more, jaw slacked, and her rhythm faltered. I sat up for only a moment to turn her over and onto her stomach, sliding into her from the back. She perked her ass up to meet my strokes, gripping my black silk sheets in her hands. Her moans were loud, we were both quite audible. The walls in my room had heard nothing like it in years, so surely our intimate act had taken the staff off guard. But like I told her, none of that mattered outside of her when I was in her. I wasn't fibbing when I told her she was my escape. She'd become that the moment she slammed into me in Times Square. The escape only got better the night we were intimate after my cousin's wedding.

I had no idea where this was going between Zoe and I but I knew where ever it went, I wanted for us to be there together.

She clung hard to me like a vise inside. I groaned from the feeling, and the surge of energy working its way up from my gut. I swooped her locs to the opposite side of her neck and pressed my lips there.

"Bryant," she whispered into my pillows. "You're so deep."

I slid my hand between her waist and my mattress in search of her clit, which she helped me find by spreading her legs.

She got louder the moment I circled my finger around her bud while thrusting in and out of her, my speed never faltering.

Her moans and my groans bounced off my gray walls, my eyes rolling to a close after she whispered, "I'm coming."

Eager to meet her arrival, knowing how much she liked that, I pumped harder, grunting with each stroke I had left to deliver. Her body shook beneath me and shook the bed too. I bucked, moaning as my seed sputtered from the head of my dick while I continued to slide in and out of her.

The recklessness of the moment added to the sensation rolling through me in waves, tingling my spine and making my head spin.

No non-disclosure. No condom. No care in the world in this moment or any moment with her. What the hell was I doing?!

It was like my good friend's death made me want to risk it all, and Zoe was who I wanted to risk it with.

I collapsed atop her and pressed my mouth to the back of her neck. She turned her face away from the pillow beneath her head, whimpering moans as I showered her neck with kisses. We laid there for a moment, completely spent. Since arriving at my mansion from the funeral and sexing in my office, we'd been sexing on and off ever since. First using our bodies, then our mouths, then back to our bodies until we laid there unmoving.

I rolled off her and onto my back. She turned on her side, brushing her locs from her face. Our eyes locked and the sex in hers made me want to pounce once more. This woman was beautiful. Not your typical beauty either. Zoe's beauty came from within and materialized on the outside as a goddess. For someone who hadn't gotten a wink of sleep, she appeared divine beside me.

She closed her eyes, and I reached toward her, caressing the side of her cheek with my hand.

"This is crazy," she said, more so to herself. "All of this is insane."

I chuckled, gliding my thumb down the fullest part of her bottom lip.

She moved in closer, pressing her hand to my chest, then eventually her head. I wrapped my arms around her and held her there in my space. Relationships have been an after thought for me. Business always before pleasure. The thing with business is when you are deep into it, pleasure is far from an option, but with Zoe, I felt like pleasure both physical and emotional was all I wanted and only with her. I could honestly stay there forever with her in my arms.

She wiggled out of my hold, though.

"Where are you going?"

"To take a shower." She grinned. "You're dripping out of me for the hundredth time."

I smiled, then licked my lips while wrapping my hand around her wrist, pulling her back toward me. "I enjoy dripping out of you."

She laughed while shaking her head. Zoe moved close again, pressing her mouth to mine and leaving a kiss. "I'll be back."

"You promise?"

"Yeah, I promise," she replied, stepping off the bed. I watched her ass sway from left to right as she made her way to the bathroom, my dick coming alive once again.

I was seconds away from hopping off my king-sized mattress and joining her in the shower when the chime of my phone in my trousers interrupted my plans. I stepped off the bed, grabbing my boxers and slipping them on before retrieving my device out of my trousers' pocket.

"Torrence," I said into the line, peeking over my shoulder toward my bathroom. The drumming of shower water cascading out of the shower head and hitting the tub floor echoed from the bathroom. "What do I owe the pleasure of receiving a call on a Sunday?"

"My apologies, Bryant," he replied. "We've been trying to get in touch with you from last week."

I shut my eyes and sighed. "Yes, I should apologize about that. A good friend of mine passed away on the 5th of this month and I needed to take some personal time off."

"Ah, sorry to hear that," Torrence replied. "I'm also sorry to bring this up now with the understanding this isn't the best time, but..." He cleared his throat. "We all are eager to move forward with the plans for the property."

"Of course," I acknowledged with a nod, my attempt at switching gears and refocusing. "Well, I've gained my grandmother's property. The paperwork is signed and in my possession so you can begin demolition plans as soon as you're ready."

"Excellent!" he stated with so much enthusiasm I couldn't help but to smile. "I'm excited to close this deal with you, Bryant."

"As am I," I replied. "Have your assistant fax to me the agreement for the property's land, and I'll sign on the dotted line. The land my grand-mother's property sits on will be yours before the spring, if all is well of course."

"And it will be. Getting on that right now!" Torrence confirmed. "It's always great doing business with you. I look forward to the history we're about to make with *The Greene Group*."

My smile grew bigger.

And I look forward to adding a few more zeros to my net worth making me the youngest billionaire in the country, I thought.

"Like music to my ears, Torrence," I replied. "We'll talk soon."

After ending the call, I sat there for a moment, smiling with all my teeth. I was reaching goals, setting records, adding bank, and had prob-ably found the woman of my dreams.

"Yes," I whispered to myself.

Things were going great for Bryant Greene.

"So that's what's wrong with you," she said behind me.

I twisted at my waist quickly, turning to her voice.

"You sold your grandmother's property, Bryant?" she asked low, just above a whisper.

My brows shot up and my jaw dropped.

"She *loves* that property." Her eyes moved off mine. "Couldn't stop talking about it with me at the wedding. She planned to visit next month to see how well you've fixed it up because... she *trusted* that with it in your hands, you would make it better than it already was."

She clutched the organic cotton towel against her breasts, her face wearing a wrinkled glare of disgust.

"It's a fucking heirloom, Bryant."

"Zoe—"

"What?"

I closed my eyes and ran my hands down my mouth completely at a loss for words.

"*What* can you possibly say right now to justify the shit I heard?"

I lifted my chin, squared my shoulders, and swallowed what confidence I had left. "The sale of the property is the best thing for—"

"You?" she interjected. "It's the best thing for *you*, right? Because don't sit there and say it's the best thing for your grandmother." Zoe stomped her way over to me. "You fucking lied to her. Straight deceived her to her face!" She shoved me on the shoulder with her free hand. "You promised you would manage the property, and she believed you. That woman who holds you in such high regard *trusted* you to do it."

"Zoe—"

"And if you could lie right to your grandmother's face, to that sweet woman's face, it would be nothing for you to be dishonest with me too."

Zoe dropped the damp towel and reached for the bra, panties, and white dress she wore the day before.

"Zoe, wait."

"Hell no," she spat, clasping her bra closed. "Rich dudes, poor dudes; y'all are all the same, just lie different. And I am *so* done with all of y'all. I swear to God! You said we were more than what we did last night, but I don't believe you. I can't believe anything you say. I'm getting the fuck out of here."

"Zoe, I'm—"

"Greedy," she gritted through her teeth as she slid on her panties and reached for her dress, poking her arms through the sleeves. She pinched the dress closed over her breasts, quickly tying the belt to hold the fabric together when she approached again. "You're a greedy green fucking snake in green grass, Greene."

I exhaled all the air in me.

"I've been racking my brain," she stated through her teeth, "trying to figure out what it was about you that left me uneasy. You're rich." She threw her hands up. "Insanely rich. You own enough, you have *every-thing*, but you want more and at the expense of breaking your grandmother's heart. Does she even know your plans to sell her property? Were you honorable enough to at least tell her?"

I dropped my head to my chest in defeat, and she scoffed.

"*Ugh*," she grunted loudly, turning away from me and stomping toward my door. "I can't even stand to look at you."

"Zoe, please, don't leave!" I padded toward her with quick steps. "Don't leave like this."

She scooped her heels up in her hand, pushing her feet into them one at a time as she pulled opened and stormed through my master bedroom's double doors. "I will give you back this dress, these shoes, and whatever else you've bought for me. I don't want none of them. I want nothing from you. I want *nothing* to do with you."

I chased her down one side of my winding staircase.

"Just give me an opportunity to explain all of this—"

"Fuck you!" she hollered, her voice echoing around the entry way.

My security emerged from the sides of my property and I raised a hand to stop them from closing in on us.

"Please, I'm fine," I said to them. "Just... go!"

"What are y'all going to do? Tackle me to the ground?!" she shouted at them when they hesitated to leave Zoe and I.

I gestured with my hands for them to go.

Her hand was on the knob of my door when I ran up to her and grabbed her by the waist to stop her. I pressed my face to the top of her head and held her tight against me. "Zoe, I am *begging you* not to leave. Please. Don't. Go."

When I turned her to face me, I noticed her face was sodden with tears. My heart broke instantly.

"Don't call me," she whispered. "Don't text me, don't even think about me. I don't want your car. I—" She rolled her eyes and her lips trembled before she took another breath. "I don't want anything to do with you, Bryant."

I felt her words pierce my chest. "*Please* let me explain."

"Let you explain how I'm sure you're selling your grandmother's property to some rich white men who want to come into one of the *first* black communities in New York and change that?" She shook her head slowly. "You're a sellout."

All I could do was stare. I bit inside my lip, trying my hardest to find the right words to say to her. To tell her whatever I needed to tell her to keep her here.

"What have you done for your people, Bryant?"

Though I've donated handsomely to causes and organizations, I couldn't with a straight face answer honestly, and whole heartedly.

"How have you helped to make the community of people who resemble you better? What tools, resources, *anything* have you given to your people so they can earn at least a crumb of what you have?"

I swallowed hard.

"Until you can answer that, don't even speak my name because that's what I'm about."

She turned to open the door and rushed out... and I let her go. The cold air slammed against my bare chest and legs as I watched her stomp down the stairs of my mansion. I gestured at my driver to open the door and to give her a ride back to the city. I needed peace of mind that she'd get home safely. Thankfully, she didn't decline my driver's invite to step into the vehicle. As I watched the car pull away, my body cold in my doorway, for the first time in my life, as *the* Bryant Greene, I felt... broke.

Thirteen

My boots sunk into the snow. The sun above beamed down like it was the first day of summer. On a Friday morning, I stalked my way to the front doors of Mane Chicks - my home away from home.

The weather that day was bitter, a little like me I guess. And really, did I not have a reason to feel how I felt?

It had been close to a month since that situation with Bryant. It's amazing how in one instance shit can go from sweet to sour. The second hookup that started in his office left me a little uneasy. But I went along with it believing what we were creating was something more than physical. It felt more than physical.

The whole way our relationship came to be, based on a lie, a deal and then the sex. How could the sex be so earth shattering and so wrong at the same time? I ran my fingers through my locs, tugging on a few rolled strands. Bryant had been calling me since that morning I stormed out of his mansion. I sent all his calls to voicemail refusing to answer, not even one phone call. I got all of his *"I'm sorry"* texts, and his *"I need to see you"* messages, and the *"we need to talk about this"* and of course the infamous *"I can explain everything"* ones too. Then there were his *"you can't keep avoiding me"* messages. He did not understand how much I could.

One afternoon, two days after I found out the reason he lied to his grandmother about me being his girlfriend, I had my friend, Denise, drive with me out to his property. Right outside the gates of his mansion, I hopped out the car he bought for me, left the keys inside of it, and had Denise drop me back home.

"The nigga you dealing with live here?!" Denise asked, her eyes wide and all over the place. We didn't even drive through the gates that day, and her awe was huge just off the man's gates.

I sucked my teeth and buckled my seatbelt around my waist, leaving her question unanswered.

She sat there for a moment, staring at me. "Zee, the shit he did couldn't have been that bad, ma."

"He's a liar."

"Sis, I knowww but—"

"I dealt with one liar for over a decade, I'm not about to make that same mistake."

"But sis." Denise peeked out the window again, her jaw dropping momentarily due to how big his property sat in the distance. "He lives in a mansion! Damnnn, look at the crib! Rocco ain't had two pennies to rub together to call change. You messing with a whole different breed. Let's be real here, all these dudes are dogs but this dog's doghouse I'm staring at is too fly! I can't let you do this. You really about to walk away from all this?"

"No," I answered, my eyes focused straight ahead. "We about to drive away from all this. Start the car already and let's get the hell out of here."

I wanted nothing to do with him then, and my feelings had yet to change.

The moment I pushed open the doors of *Mane Chicks*, my eyes shot over to my booth where red roses flooded the area. These floral arrangements like the ones Bryant left at the doorstep of my apartment were different. The stems were extra long, and there were several dozens bundled as one. At the salon around my booth, some sat in super large crystal vases, five of them, while one bunch laid on the leather chair in front of my booth.

I rolled my eyes closed as I walked closer.

"Girl!" Meesha, one of the stylist at *Mane Chicks*, gushed from her seat. "These roses are next level. I ain't never seen flowers like these before and baby I done seen plenty of flowers in this lifetime."

"*Mm-hmm*," I replied. I pulled off my coat and hooked it on the rack near the door.

"They *are* gorgeous," Vita, another stylist complimented. If her eyes could mimic the shape of hearts, her pupils would be flooded with them in that moment.

I approached the flowers and moved a few of the vases to the side with my foot to make way for myself. Lifted the bundle of roses on the chair, then dropped them to the floor.

Gasps rang out around me.

"Zoe!" Shia, the shop's owner, rasped from the front desk. She always sat there every morning, arranging appointments and handling the business side of the shop since she didn't work from a back office. "What the hell you doing?"

I plugged in my thermal styling kit and turned to face her while pulling my locs up to the top of my head. "If you like 'em so much, y'all can have 'em. Have all of them. I don't care."

Her head slowly jerked back as she leaned back in her seat. "And what the hell wrong with you?" she asked loud. Shia's voice was deeper than it should have been for a woman, but it was the one thing I loved the most about her. She was like a mother to me and the only maternal figure I had in my life besides my girl, Joi's, grandmother. I never knew my mother or met my blood family on my mother's or father's side. My mother gave me up for adoption the day I was born. When I was 14, I found her name in an adoption database and reached out. She wanted nothing to do with me at birth or as a teen, so that was that on that. Growing up in foster care and moving from home to home, I wasn't a stranger to not having many solid relationships. So when I met Shia when I was 19-years-old, while she shopped at a local beauty supply store where I worked as a cashier, we clicked and I made sure to maintain and nurture our friendship. I treasured Shia. She knew me better than everyone else at the shop, better than almost everyone in my life, besides my best friend Joi. So I knew I wouldn't need to explain too much.

"I had a similar batch of flowers sent to my apartment," I explained matter-of-factly as I slid on my Mane Chicks-branded apron and dusted off my chair with the cape draped over my chair. "And they went right in the incinerator. These will do the same so if y'all like them so much, come get 'em."

Most of the women were up and out of their seats, rushing my way like my area was Walmart at midnight on Black Friday.

"Aye!" Shia shouted, shooting up from her seat. "If any of you touch her flowers, I swear on everything I'mma snatch sew-ins left and right. Don't y'all put one hand on that girl's roses. They are *hers*. Sit y'all thirsty asses down somewhere."

"She doesn't want them," Vita argued.

"I said what I said," Shia replied. "Zoe, come over here, let me talk to you."

I rolled my eyes and closed the space between us. Now standing over her desk directly opposite her, she turned her palms up to face me, asking me what was up without actually asking it.

"They're from a nigga I shouldn't be gettin' them from."

Her eyes ballooned. "Rocco sent these?!"

I shook my head. "Nah, some other dude."

"Drug dealer?"

"Might as well be," I answered.

Shia leaned in, resting most of her weight on the desk below her. "Zoe, what this man do to piss you off like this? He hit you? Because if this fool hit you, I will—"

"No, he didn't hit me."

"Then what he do?"

I turned my chin to my shoulder to focus out of the shop, not at all interested in going into the details.

"I mean, whatever he did, he's clearly very sorry about it." She gestured at the flowers. "He's gone out of his way to show it and I'm sure he has told you it too."

"I can't do shit with his sorry Shia." I focused on her again. "Sorry can't erase most things."

"Understandable." She glanced at the other ladies before making eye contact with me again. "So you're not going to tell me what he did, huh? Just gon' have these women in here jack you for all your flowers because you mad at the fool who did something wrong but not wrong enough for you to put him on blast?"

I shrugged.

"If he's not a drug dealer, what does the brother do? 'Cause these flowers right here, without needing to see a price tag, are more than expensive, love. They look rare. And for him to send so many..."

I ran my tongue over my teeth and said nothing.

Shia giggled in her seat. "Well, whatever this man has done to you, it must have been terrible. He fucked up in a major way because not only are you not dragging him, naming him, or accepting anything from him, but you standing here sadder than a cloudy day. That's not the Zoe I know. You actually look sadder than you did after that shit with Rocco, and you and Rocco got years between y'all. You just met this new guy! What's up?"

"*This* guy..." I sighed, checking over my shoulder at the ladies, then leaning closer to Shia and lowering my voice. "This guy made me fall *hard* and *fast* for him, Shia. He tapped into a side of me I didn't even know was there. Made me think he was one way when he wasn't. Yeah, he got money, but he's a disappointment. I thought he was different, the exception. It's clear to me now that no matter where they grow up or who raised them, a fuck boy is going to be a fuck boy, regardless. There're just levels to it, you know?"

"Hmph," Shia huffed. "Baby, if there's anyone who *knows*, it's me."

I scoffed a laugh.

"I ain't gon' let these ladies take your roses though, Zoe. These are *yours*. He might have fucked up, but the flowers stay here or go home with you. Those are the only options." Her eyes wandered over to the roses when she sighed at the sight of them. "They really are beautiful, Zo."

"They are. And I would keep them if they didn't remind me so much of him." I turned to glance at the flowers again, forcing myself not to swoon. "That's one thing he's good at, selecting the best."

"I agree." Shia grinned. "He chose you."

But did he?

The only reason he and I got as far as we did was because one, I lost my cool behind the wheel of my car and two, because he knew he could use me as a result of that. So did he really *choose* me? Or did my circumstances do all the work?

I twisted my lips to one side and shrugged. "If only that were true."

Fourteen

BRYANT

I sat in the backseat of the black SUV, staring out at the salon to my right. I'd heard Zoe mention frequently the name of the hair parlor and having to go there to meet her clients.

We hadn't spoken in a month. My phone calls to her had gone unanswered, texts marked as *read* but not replied to. I'd even resorted to sending her flowers, hoping they would at least force her to give me a call to thank me for them. But... nothing.

Unfortunately, this wasn't one of those situations with the women in my past where I could brush our falling out off and move on. I couldn't get Zoe out of my mind. Not only was she an exceptional woman, she offered me something I couldn't find in everyone - an opportunity to feel normal and at ease. The blessing of trusting someone other than myself.

That afternoon, for instance, I wanted to drive out to her salon alone, but my head of security told me it would be a bad idea. My name was more recognizable than I was by design, but my head of security, Paul, informed me the area wouldn't be safe enough for me to travel there solo. The only regular car I owned didn't even belong to me. It was Zoe's, and I hated the way it drove over New York City's roads, so there was no way I would use it as a mode of transportation that day.

When security alerted me to her being outside the property a few weeks back, my heart smiled. I thought she'd returned for us to talk after not answering my calls or my texts. But once I received a second notification she'd arrived on the property with another unidentifiable vehicle and had left her car and driven off in the other car, my heart sank. She really made it clear she wanted nothing to do with me, and I had no idea how to repair the damage I created.

I hadn't thought this far; I hadn't planned for *this*. My plans were all in getting my grandmother's property, closing the deal, and adding the necessary 0s to my account to facilitate my goals. Then Zoe slammed into me in Times Square and everything changed. Everything.

So much so, I was sitting outside a salon in Brownsville. A part of town I'd never been to, and knew nothing about, but according to Paul, Brownsville was the inner-city and wasn't safe for a man like me.

My eyes roamed around the area. Loose trash sat atop caps of snow, some litter blowing in the wind. The buildings were a bit decrepit, one or two dilapidated, some businesses having planks of wood on their window frames instead of glass. Individuals, mostly men, dressed from head to toe in streetwear, stood outside stores talking or smoking cigarettes.

I'd never exposed myself to this side of life. I've seen it on TV, watched a few shows and movies in the past that have captured parts of this life, but I had never *seen* it in person before.

Zoe's last words to me in front of the door of my property continued to play on in my mind. The men interested in acquiring my grandmother's property faxed over the paperwork and agreements had been sitting on my desk for the past few weeks waiting for my signature, but I couldn't bring myself to do it.

I stroked my fingers through the hairs on my beard and turned to peer out the window once again.

"Sir?" Paul asked from the front seat. "Whenever you're ready."

"Yes," I replied, gliding my palm down my brown wool coat. Mindful of where I was going, I did my best to dress down. Instead of my usual suit, I opted for a wool coat, cable-knit rolled neck sweater, a pair of jeans, and Chelsea boots. I had to see her. Our first stop was at her apartment building. To send her the flowers, I had to use the help of my driver to get her address. On this day, I stopped there before driving to the salon, but there was no answer when I buzzed her bell outside the building. I hoped like hell she'd be in the salon today.

The second I pushed opened the car door, the cold air brushed against my face. Paul was out of the SUV immediately, making his way over to me, and pulling the door open wider for me to step out. He insisted on having a crew of security with us, so they traveled in the car behind us. The moment my boots touched the snowy pavement, they were all out, standing a few feet from the salon's front door. Paul would be the only one to walk in with me, I insisted on that. And I'm glad I did, because after seeing how small inside the salon was, there was no way having five bulky close to seven feet tall men present would work in the tiny space.

"Well, good afternoon," a busty woman with a deep-pitched voice greeted at the front desk of the salon. She was out of her seat the second the salon's door closed behind Paul.

I flashed her a smile, and she returned one back that was bigger than mine.

"Good afternoon," I voiced, my eyes traveling around the salon, searching for a familiar face. "Is Zoe in?"

Her eyes grew wide. "And you are...?"

"A friend," I replied. As I stated, my name was more recognizable than my face and I wasn't interested in attracting any unwanted attention.

The woman's big eyes drifted past me to see Paul, who stood by the front door on guard. Her view moved through the doors to outside. I turned to glance that way and saw my guards standing only a few feet from the door, literally surrounding the area.

"Are you the friend who bought her all those flowers?"

I chuckled. "Guilty."

"Interesting choice of words," she rasped as she took a seat behind the front desk again.

My eyes moved past her and to the other women in the shop who all seemed fixed on me. I smiled, and a few swooned in their seats.

"Well, I'm Shia," she introduced below me, drawing my attention back on her. "I'm the owner of this shop."

"It's a lovely salon."

"Why, thank you!" she blushed. "Zoe is like a daughter to me. Met her when she was 19 and she's been working here from the time she was 21-years-old."

I hiked my brows. "Impressive. She's very talented."

"Extremely," Shia added. "And very smart."

"That she is." I leaned my forearm against the top of the high desk.

"May I give a suggestion regarding her?"

I gestured with my hands for Shia to continue. "Please."

She leaned in and in a lower throaty voice told me, "Whatever you did that's got her so pissed with you, beautiful roses ain't gon' cut it."

"Uh-huh?" I tucked my lips into my mouth and moved in closer. "She's not into flowers?"

"She's not into bullshit."

I snorted a laugh, suddenly a fan of Shia's no holds barred attitude. "I see."

"Mm-hmm."

"So then." I moved in even closer. "What do you suggest I do? Because I really lov—" I paused, surprising myself. Shia's brows went up and I cleared my throat in response. "I really *admire* Zoe and enjoy her company a lot. And she's not returning my phone calls or replying to any of my messages and I..." I turned to peek over at Paul who still stood at the door. "I just *need* to talk to her and explain myself."

"Well..." Shia sighed. "She won't tell me what you did, and the fact that you're also speaking in code is proof enough you don't plan to tell me either."

I blinked once.

"But whatever you did wasn't no superficial thing because she's still trying to protect you. She had a boyfriend not too long ago who did some dog shit to her," Shia revealed through her teeth. "She came in here the next day dragging his ass, did it for *days* on end. But with you, she hasn't spoken a single negative thing, not a single one which means she *admires* you as much as you admire her."

I smiled.

"But you hurt her in a way that'll take more than you buying her something. You understand what I'm saying to you?"

My smile melted into a frown.

"You got to *think* here. And you seem to be very smart, so this shouldn't be too hard."

"*Hmm*," I hummed. "Not smart enough not to mess this up with her."

"She's leaving the door open for you. Zoe is not about to make it easy, though. You can't buy her. That girl has always been that way. She's used to not having a lot and needs little to be happy. I love that the most about her." Shia leaned back in her chair. "Nah, if you're really sorry, and you want to get back in good with her, you got to do something from the heart to show Zoe you are worthy of having hers, you get me?"

I moved my eyes off Shia's and focused them down on the top of the desk, thinking.

When the thought popped in my head, my brows shot up and I offered a closed-mouth smile. "Yes, I do, actually."

I met my eyes with hers again. "Shia, you've been a lot of help."

"I know."

I chuckled.

"And by the way..." She leaned in again. "I enjoyed that article on you in *For The Culture* a few years ago."

I arched a brow.

"*Mm-hmm*, I *know* who you are, Mr. Greene. I can't be a successful business owner in this country without knowing who all the elite business connoisseurs are."

A laugh escaped my mouth, which I tried to suppress by tucking my lips in.

"You're a dope brother." She peeked to her right. "The rest of these ladies in here may not understand how dope you are because they're more familiar with the entertainers and the like who wear their wealth and flaunt their new money, but you're the one making the real moves out here. But you could make better ones, which is probably what you and Zoe fell out about."

"You're good," I said low. "Really good."

She smiled big. "Oh, I know."

"Sir?" Paul called behind me.

"Another moment, Paul," I replied, aware he was alerting me it was time to go.

"You fix this, hear?" Shia insisted below me. "That girl deserves you. Show her you deserve her too."

"Yes, ma'am." I extended my hand out to shake hers. "I appreciate your time."

"Oh, child, it was nothing," she explained, accepting my hand with both of hers.

I glanced at the stack of business cards on the desk and took one. In her view, I held the card up and tucked it in my coat's inside pocket.

She pressed her hand to her chest. "Thank you!"

"No," I replied, turning my feet toward the shop's exit. "Thank you."

FIFTEEN

The phone calls finally stopped... the ones from Bryant. So did the texts. I woke up that morning in a bad funk and I couldn't understand why. Called out and rescheduled all of my clients for Monday appointments. Stayed in bed two hours after waking.

It didn't occur to me why my mood plummeted until my mind drifted back to a time I was at my happiest. The night of Bryant's cousin's wedding at the castle. The trip down memory lane left me with thoughts of him. They were like residue I struggled to wipe off my fingers... but I didn't want to rub him off.

Around three in the afternoon, I decided I needed to hit the market to buy a few groceries for my fridge. The way I felt made it clear I wouldn't be going anywhere that weekend. So I loaded my shopping cart up on two large pints of chocolate ice cream, pretzels, dried mangoes, poultry, rice, and vegetables. Figured if I cook one enormous meal, snack, and sleep the rest of the time, I'd get over whatever this was.

Was I missing him?

Nah, impossible. I stopped answering his calls and replying to his messages for a reason. He proved to be a snake, a liar. Took the trust of his grandmother and was about to ruin their relationship over money. The man I thought I knew was a figment of my imagination.

He wasn't real.

What he showed to me wasn't real. His good heart was a game. Excellent game. And I'd fallen hard, like an idiot.

I scoffed as I made my way down the block toward my apartment.

I replayed the moment at his mansion when I overheard him talking on the phone. Literally took a quick shower with plans to climb back in the bed with him so we could do what we'd been doing the entire night before. Then I overheard him discussing his grandmother's property. I made my way closer to the bathroom's door to listen in, and what I heard broke my heart. The one thing I admired him for - taking on the responsibility of his grandmother's property - wasn't going to happen. I found it noble of him, to take on something as small as an ancient property when he had so many other things to focus on. Only to discover the shit came with a catch. I hated the dishonesty. It made me question everything he told me, including his promise we were more than the hookups. I needed to believe we were. My heart sure felt that way.

I thought I hated him. Then why was my ass thinking about him heavily when he'd finally given me what I wanted? I wanted him to leave me alone, and he stopped calling and texting me for a whole week. So why was my mood like this?

The moment I turned the corner to continue up the way to my apartment building, I spotted a few tall men standing near the perimeter of my building. My brows wrinkled as I trekked closer, and those same brows shot up when I recognized one of the men.

"Paul?" I asked to more so myself.

Seeing him made me search for another familiar face, and I didn't need to search far.

He stood feet away, his eyes already on me. I froze in place, my hands clutching the handles of my grocery bags.

Bryant leaned against the silver Camry I left outside the gates of his mansion weeks ago. He buried his hands in the pockets of his slacks. His camel wool coat laid opened at his sides, pulled back by his arms, a black cashmere sweater in full view. The man just oozed elegance without even trying.

He pushed his back off the car and stood tall.

"What are you doing here?" I asked as I made my way over to him.

"I drove your car," he revealed, ignoring my question. "The vehicle drives just as horribly as it did when you test drove it, if not worse."

I snickered, dropping my head to hide my smile. His comment reminded me of what he complained about when I decided on the car I wanted. We went for a test drive and he was less than impressed. Tried like hell to influence me to change my mind for something else, a luxury vehicle he promised I'd love more, but I wanted *this* car. There was no way I planned to park a fancy car on this block. The car would probably get jacked for its parts hours after I left it unattended. I needed something to blend in with. Plus...

"I like it," I admitted out loud.

"I like *you*," he said next. "I..." He peeked at Paul and the rest of the men before returning his eyes on me. "I love you."

I released the breath I'd been holding. The one I felt caught in my chest since that morning. Bryant made his way over to me, his scent reaching me before he did. I closed my eyes and inhaled deep, missing his smell, his aura. He did a fucked up thing, but my mind, body, and soul had trouble understanding that.

His hands were at the handles of the market's plastic bags as he removed them from my grip. He held them out for Paul to take, which Paul did without question. And I didn't protest. I couldn't.

I love you, kept swarming through my head. Did he just say that? Or did I imagine the words?

"I love you, Zoe," he avowed again, this time cradling my jaw in his hands. "You were right. What I planned to do was snakish, wrong, underhanded, and *definitely* greedy."

My eyes darted along his face.

"That's why I didn't go through with the deal."

Bryant took my hand and walked me to my car. "I have other plans for the property, plans my grandmother approves of and is excited to see come to fruition."

"Other plans?" I mustered up.

"Indeed." He flashed that brilliant smile of his. "Condominiums that offer affordable housing for people who've fallen on hard times."

My heart leaped.

"I've done some research on this area." He glanced around himself.

"There are quite a few new buildings going up and many current buildings being demolished displacing a lot of residents. The situation helped me come up with a solution to a growing issue."

"Gentrification."

"Correct." He licked his lips. "Because of that, I've decided to invest in a few projects, one of which is to buy and renovate properties, creating luxury apartments that offer affordable housing. Another project will focus on temporary housing for the homeless, housing that can transition to something permanent. I have a plan to house residents in another property who have been displaced until they can get back on their feet." He took a breath. "My ideas are still in their infancy stages, but I sure could use your help with them."

Bryant brushed his thumb down my lip and I closed my eyes at his touch.

"I need you in my life, Zoe."

I hadn't even realized how much I missed him or his touch until that moment.

"Somehow, some way, I've fallen in love with you, and..." He exhaled. "I'm tired of trying to figure out why or even how it happened. I want you and I need you to forgive me for my past decisions. They came from a place I'm less than proud of these days."

"I don't know what to say," I replied. And I really didn't. This was all so sudden. Everything moved so fast. It was hard believing this wasn't a dream.

"You make me feel normal, good," he told me. "That's one reason Lennox and I hit it off the moment we met. Through all this," he said, gesturing at himself. "He saw *me* and somehow you see even more of me and I love that. I *love* you."

A smile spread across my lips. "You said it again."

"I'll say those words a million more times if that's what it will take for you to know what I'm saying is real and from my heart." He moved in even closer. "Zoe, I'm in love with you."

I glanced around us. The block was quiet, so Bryant's security appearing out of place wasn't hard to see.

I laughed at the sight. "This is crazy."

"Give me another shot."

I turned to him again. "Another shot? You want another shot... with... me?"

"We can take things slow if you prefer. Dinner, movie dates, possibly trips? Let's start from scratch."

My head was spinning. Was this really happening? And this soon?

It was, and just like Bryant, I wasn't interested in fighting these feelings or trying to make sense of them either.

He stepped back and extended his hand for me to take. "Hi, I'm Bryant Greene. You are?"

"In love too," I answered, honestly.

He exhaled all the air he held in him, dropping his head back between his shoulders with relief.

"Oh thank God, " he whispered at the sky.

Bryant leveled his head to meet my eyes again.

I moved in closer, balancing myself on the arches of my feet, and wrapping my arms around the back of his neck. He crushed his lips against mine and coiled his arms tight around me. His mouth against mine was such a missed sensation. Soft and full enough to cover mine, I melted in his embrace.

"Nice to meet you," I whispered on his lips.

Epilogue
Manhattan, December 2021

BRYANT

I leaned back in my chair, eyes fixed to the architectural model in front of me. The designers of said model completed the structure for my office building years ago, so it was an easy decision who to call once I began planning the infrastructure for my upcoming building project.

Another building structure they designed, the one in Morgansville and that they built on land that my grandmother entrusted in me, was flourishing. New applicants came in daily to interview for a spot to take residence there. Currently, we had seven families in the ten unit building and were interviewing more candidates.

The investors for the original deal weren't too happy when I informed them I was backing out of their plans. They even tried to have the new project I had planned for my grandmother's land halted, with attempts to tie me up in useless paperwork and lawsuits right around construction time. Like all other obstacles, I didn't accept defeat, nor did I believe it was an option. Plus with Zoe at my side, constantly reassuring me that I made the best decision and that everything would work out in my favor because I was doing things with the right frame of mind and heart, I proceeded with plans to build and today the results surpassed even my expectations.

"Sir?" Chelsea asked at the door.

I swiveled my chair in that direction to glance that way. She stood at the threshold, her short black pixie cut hair freshly trimmed, black pantsuit perfectly pressed, as her brow arched for permission to enter.

"Come on in, Chelsea."

She bowed her head and stepped in, her eyes landing on the model on my desk. Chelsea pointed and asked, "Is this the design for the second building project?"

"Yes it is," I answered, smiling with pride. "Specifically for the affordable housing program."

"It's exquisite." She took a seat. "Very luxurious."

"Only the best." I adjusted the direction of my tie.

"Speaking of which…" She opened up her folder and pulled out a printed sheet. "These are the list of approved amenities set in place for this property. You plan to build in Brooklyn, correct?"

"Yes, Brownsville."

"Gotcha."

After much thought regarding where I would build, Zoe proposed Brownsville for one property. With all the new buildings going up and old buildings being torn down, she thought it would be a perfect place for displaced families who could afford it, to have an option of remaining in the neighborhood they've lived all their lives.

"Where are you planning to put the art studio for the neighborhood kids?"

I pointed at the lower level portion of the model. "Here."

Her eyes lit up.

"Have we heard from the street muralist?"

"Yes," Chelsea bobbled her head. "Naazir Goodman, that's his name, has agreed to volunteer his time to not only create the artwork for the space once we build the building, but to teach the youth once every week."

"Perfect."

"He asked for us to let him know an estimated date for when he would have to begin."

"We will keep him posted."

"So on the schedule for next week," she began, "Is the Buy The Block Back celebration dinner, honoring you and your first masterclass at the center."

"Excellent."

At the insistence of Zoe, I'd donated five million to Buy The Block Back, a non-for-profit organization created to teach business management workshops to inner-city residents. Zoe's friend's husband, Jeremiah Rhames, interestingly enough started it. We'd had them over at the mansion earlier in the year and attended their garden wedding this past summer. I loved his enthusiasm for the program. So much so, not only did I donate money, I agreed to donate my time too, giving business advice to the brothers and sisters in the community along with mentorship when they opened their own business, preferably within the inner-city. The plan was to guide them through their first year of business to assist with building confidence and the knowledge on how to plan, execute, and maintain a thriving business.

"How's construction going for Ms. Stewart's salon?"

Chelsea blushed. "Really well. She called an hour ago to let you know she'll be running a little late getting on the tarmac at your estate because of it. She's reviewing mirrors for the walls and the glasses for outside the shop."

I smiled. "Not a problem. She's so hands on."

"That she is. She's giving orders like a pro out there." Chelsea winked.

I laughed to myself. "What else is there?"

"We have to arrange for a visit to *Greene Gardens*. In the new year would be best, spring preferably, when all the snow has melted."

Greene Gardens.

After a lengthy conversation with Zoe, where I complained about the stalling that had occurred after backing out of the deal with the investors who wanted my grandmother's property, Zoe asked, matter-of-factly, why I couldn't build my own community.

I thought the idea was too far fetched until I researched it and learned there were several acres of land for sale, available right here in New York State. So I placed a bid and acquired 410 acres of land. Not much, but a good start in building something for the people... as Zoe put it.

I had plans to make Greene Gardens a metropolis, made up of thriving black-owned businesses and a focused-based community with a mindset of constructing and maintaining our own. Our slogan we'd settled on was "where black businesses and black communities come to grow."

"A lottery for business owners and potential residents is underway," Chelsea announced. "We've gotten quite a few applicants so far."

"Very good."

The plans were in the infancy stages, but I was beyond excited for what was to come.

"Finally." Chelsea smiled. "I've cleared your schedule for the rest of the week for your getaway."

I bobbed my head. "The private jet?"

"Gassed with the crew already on board, ready when you're ready to fly out, sir." She stifled a scream, and I had to chuckle at her enthusiasm.

"Chelsea..."

"I apologize, sir, but I am *so* excited. I cannot *wait* until next Monday when I see Zoe and can get all the details."

I laughed, rubbing my hands together. "I'm sure Zoe will have a lot to tell once we return."

———

ZOE

Ocean waves crashing against sturdy rocks woke me. I stirred against the silk sheets, my hand sliding over the smooth fabric in search of him.

We'd arrived just as the sun was setting. I'd fallen asleep on the G550, my eyes peeling open the moment the private jet's wheels skidded against the island's tarmac. He was the first person I saw when I awoke on the plane, a smile pulling at the corners of his mouth.

"You'll get more rest at the villa, promise," he told me before I could apologize for not being much company on the way over.

St. Barts was the destination. A week prior, Bryant insisted that we take a brief break. Put aside all projects for a few days and just head to the island for a little R&R, as he put it. I didn't give him any pushback because truthfully, I needed this.

I'd been the little birdy in his ear this past year. After going on and on about how he needed to give back, leave a real legacy by helping people who resembled him get even an ounce of what he had, he put me on the job. He felt my ear was more to the community than his. He told me to name the place and he would donate either money, his time, or both. In the process, he thought it was time for me to have my own too. So he insisted on buying an entire commercial property for me to house my own salon and for me to rent out space to other business owners too. I agreed, so long as Shia could be a partner in my salon. Mane Chicks was my second home, and I owed so much to her for taking me on when I'd just started out with nothing. My salon, Zoe's Beauty Lounge, had the best of both worlds. With Shia's partnership, I could offer hair services, makeup, and beauty consultations. I was working on getting my girl Joi to set up shop in one of the building spaces to offer her services in her own boutique spa. There was still a way to go for *Zoe's Beauty Lounge* to be up and running, but I'd been pouring a lot of my energy into it as if we were opening its doors tomorrow.

Speaking of doors...

It seems whenever you're moving confidently into your future, the past has a way with trying to see if its keys still work.

"What up, Zee?"

I stood over a spread of marble floor tile samples that laid on a wooden table when his voice stole my attention.

"Wow," Rocco said, his eyes big with fascination as his head moved from left-to-right taking in the raw space of my new salon. "Zoe, this spot is huge, baby. Damn!"

Workers from an awning supplier installed an awning with my shop's name just that morning, so I was on a natural high. Rocco almost threatened that joy by popping up out of nowhere.

I was of course opening my salon in Brooklyn. Joi had already told me she'd run into Rocco around the way a few months earlier and that she told him all about my new life and relationship with Bryant. Well, actually, she threw the news of me moving on in Rocco's face, rubbed my new relationship in until he bared his teeth and stomped off. My girl always keeps her word.

Anyway, the streets were talking, so I'm sure news of my new business spread amongst the people I knew like everything else about me these days. The fresh gossip eventually landed in Rocco's ear. But I was definitely not expecting him to have the audacity to show up uninvited. His presence stunned me. We hadn't seen each other since that day outside of my apartment building.

When he popped up unannounced at my salon, he wore his mechanic uniform. Grease covered him from his collar to his stained construction boots. And when he was close, I could smell the workday all over him.

Rocco wore the most superficial smile I'd ever seen on him. I don't think he'd ever smiled with so much teeth with me, but that day he did.

"This all you, Zee? Like, this whole thing?"

I tilted my head to my right.

"This is real nice." He nodded while stroking his chin. "You big ballin' now, huh? Done came up, for real. Look at you. Skin all glowing, designer boots shining, body looking tight and right. Out here smelling like money!"

He stepped forward. Rocco really caught himself trying to reach for my hand.

I took two steps back from him.

"Yo, I miss you so much, Zee," he tried. "You looking real good. I see you living right these days, like we always planned to when we were younger—"

"Rocco," I finally interjected. "You're dull, and everything you're saying right now is dull too. This conversation as a whole is wack, sweetheart. Sound familiar?"

He forced out a nervous chuckle. "Come on, Zoe. You know I was just playing with you when I said that—"

"And right now, you're playing in my face. You miss me? That's convenient." I folded my arms over my chest. "Please know the feeling is not

mutual." I gestured around me. "As you can see, I've moved on, and I guess I should thank you for leaving when and how you did."

"You still salty off that shit?" He scoffed a laugh. "Damn, Zoe. You gotta let that go. I ain't even with that girl no more—" Rocco paused and his jaw dropped next.

I heard footsteps approaching behind me. Without even looking I knew who it was from the way Rocco's eyes grew two sizes bigger, watching as the person approached me from behind.

"Everything okay over here?" Bryant asked, wrapping an arm around me when he was close.

"Bryant motherfucking Greene!" Rocco exhaled in awe. "Man, I can't believe you're here right now! Yo, when I found out you and Zoe..."

Bryant peeked down at me in the middle of Rocco's groupie rambling and I looked up his way. I leaned in and said, "This is Rocco."

Bryant examined me for a moment. He shifted his eyes off mine to focus on Rocco again. I thought the smile Rocco wore with me was big. The Kodak cheesing he was doing with Bryant couldn't compare.

"It's a pleasure to meet you, for real." Rocco stepped forward with his hand extended.

Bryant peered down at Rocco's outstretched hand for a few beats. His eyes met Rocco's again when he said, "I'm sure."

I'd told Bryant everything about my relationship with Rocco. When Rocco and I started dating and why we broke up. I even told Bryant about my last run in with Rocco, so Bryant was all caught up. I knew as cordial as Bryant could be, he wasn't at all interested in meeting Rocco on any level.

Instead of ever shaking Rocco's hand, Bryant said, "Paul?"

His head security guard along with another security team member approached.

"Please escort this gentleman off the premises," Bryant ordered.

The smile Rocco wore slid off his lips instantly.

"What?!" Rocco spat.

"And please," Bryant added, "have at least two men assigned to the front doors at all times to keep away any future trespassing."

"Trespassing?!" Rocco questioned. "I'm trespassing now? Yo, Zee, you gon' let—"

"Thank you, Paul," was all I said before flipping a few locs over my shoulder and turning my back to Rocco. I wrapped my arms around Bryant's waist and gazed up at him. "And thank you so much, baby."

Rocco fussed at security the whole way to the exit, and I couldn't help but to laugh to myself. I didn't even bother glancing his way as security forced him out, back on the street where he belonged. They weren't lying when they said success and falling in love with better was the most satisfying middle finger to a trifling ass ex.

"So I was thinking," I said over the echoes of Rocco's fussing. "Ethiopian food for lunch?"

"Hmm." Bryant bent his legs at the knees to press his lips to mine. "I was thinking of having you for lunch."

I tossed my head back and giggled, definitely loving the sound of that.

That was a few weeks ago. I chuckled to myself, recalling how good it felt having my future slam the door on my past.

Tonight, I turned over to my right to train my eyes past a different door. Through this door was a beach and a table for two set up on the sand. The candle light dancing with the gentle night breeze was beautiful from where I laid. I sat up, grabbing the white net hoodie I placed on the ottoman at the foot of the canopy bed before falling asleep.

When we arrived, I was so sure that I would hit the beach as soon as we dropped our luggage off. Bryant had rented a private island for our getaway, so we had the entire beachfront to ourselves. The thing was, as soon as I arrived there, changed into my black string bikini, and I laid on the bed just to relax for a bit, I fell asleep. Long enough for night to arrive.

I approached the billowing white curtains, peeling them apart to stride through. My pink pedicured toes sunk into the warm white sand as I closed the space between us. I saw him sitting in the chair, his attention out on the ocean that resembled a moving black blanket. I moved my eyes overhead to marvel at the cluster of stars sparkling in the sky and sighed at the sight.

His head turned my way instantly, a smile taking residence on his lips next. "Goodnight sleepy head."

I moaned as I stretched and he stood from his seat to approach me.

"Why didn't you wake me?"

"You needed your rest," he explained in front of me, pushing a few of my locs over my shoulder.

"But this is a getaway," I whined. "I wasn't trying to sleep the first few hours we got here."

"You're up in time to eat." Bryant took my hand, lifting it to his lips to kiss. "Come and join me."

As he escorted me, I swooned at the view of his bare back muscles. Strong and refined, my man was all that and then some.

Our relationship had been a beautiful union mixed with passion, love, and business. Bryant included me in a lot of his property work these days, especially the ones he's dedicated charity work to. It was always flattering when he asked me for my opinion on something that had anything to do with business. When I'd tell him I have no idea about business, he'd tell me what he desired was my input on how his business moves would benefit the community.

The community.

That term had become synonymous with Bryant Greene and I couldn't love him anymore for it. Bryant had become the most charitable billionaire in the country, and the youngest. He donated more than he's ever done in his career and as a result earned double what he gave. He seemed to reap the benefits even more now than he's ever before.

In front of the table, Bryant pulled out my chair and waited for me to take a seat before pushing the chair in as best he could against the sand.

He asked, "Do you know what today is?"

I raised the rim of my champagne glass to my lips to sip. "December 16th."

"*Mm-hmm...*" he replied, leaning back in his seat, his fingers forming a steeple around his mouth.

After staring at him for a beat, noticing the grin on his lips, it hit me. I closed my eyes and smiled. "I can't believe you remember the day we first met."

"How couldn't I?" He laughed. "It was also the day I got the bill for how much it would cost to repair my *McAlister*."

I tossed my napkin at him and his laugh grew louder. I couldn't help but to join in.

"It was one of the best days of my life," he revealed with a grin.

I blushed and looked toward the water.

When I turned to focus back on him, I noticed the ring glittering from his pinky finger.

There was no need to squint. The emerald-cut diamond was so big, I swore I needed sunglasses to shield my eyes from the way the stone winked at me beneath the moonlight. The diamond itself was a distraction. Add to that the smaller diamonds that crowded the emerald stone and covered the entire ring, even the band of the white gold, its presence left me completely blinded by the shine.

"Oh my God. Bryant!"

He rose from his seat, sporting just a pair of black swim trunks. Made his way over to me and lowered down on one knee, his eyes never leaving mine.

"I want to make this day an even better day than it was two years ago."

"Whoa."

"You are more than a woman to me, you're my partner. And though love is very important in marriage, a union with someone with strong morals and ethics in life and business is a must for me since marriage is also a business..."

I tilted my head to the right. "Bryant, what the hell kind of proposal is this?"

He bellowed a laugh, and I snickered, rolling my eyes.

"The romantic part is coming right now, love of my life. I can promise you that."

I giggled.

"I love you with everything in me. You're without a doubt my better half," he continued. "I'm so much more whole with you in my corner, and I'm grateful that you've chosen to be with me. You're at the top for me, the best I've ever accomplished, and it would be an honor for you to bear my last name."

I dipped my chin, my eyes welling with tears.

"How was that?" He grinned. "Was that better?"

I swiped my finger beneath my eyes. "Yes, much better, baby."

He smiled and moved in closer. "Zoe Stewart, will you do me the honor of being my wife, my lover, and my partner for the rest of our lives?"

My head was bobbing before I could think to do so, the tears streaming down my eyes next. "Yes, Mr. Greene, I absolutely will."

He slid the ring down my ring finger, lighting up my hand while weighing it down.

I swore my hand was anchored to my thigh with the ring on. And no matter how still my finger remained, the moonlight danced on the stones, making them sparkle at every angle.

I sighed in awe. "Bryant, baby, this ring is *too* much. How many carats is this? 100?"

He chuckled. "22.35 carats. There are at least 200 diamonds surrounding the stone with about 79 emeralds on the back of the band."

I lifted my bottom lip long enough to tell him, "Yup, this is *way* too much. Bryant—"

He leaned in close, pressing his soft lips to mine, causing me to lose my focus for only a moment.

"No wife of mine will wear anything less," he boasted on my lips. "So you're just going to have to deal, beautiful. I'm not compromising on this."

I pressed my palm to his cheek, and he moved his lips in that direction to leave a kiss there.

"Honestly," he said in front of me, "I would have gone bigger, but I thought it be wise that you at least be able to bend that finger, Mrs. Greene."

Mrs. Greene. I liked the sound of that. Only, this Greene was all about nourishment instead of greedy profit, and the man I planned to spend the rest of my life with was about the same thing.

"Come here." I curved my index finger, beckoning him to me. And he didn't hesitate to meet me halfway for a kiss.

"I love you," I professed on his lips.

"And I love you," he replied, sliding me closer and deeper into our kiss.

I thought I'd hit the wrong car two years ago. But it turns out I hit the car that changed my life for the better. Some would call it luck, but to me, it was the life that had always been waiting for me. And I was prepared to live it to the fullest with my man and his love that I never saw coming.

THE END.

Author's Note

Dear Reader,

Thank you for reading book three, *GREED*, in the *Love Is Cure, Vol. 1 – Vices & Virtues* series. I wrote this story in 2019 along with the other first two books in the series. To say I enjoyed penning *GREED* from start to finish would be an understatement. Bryant was truly a piece of work and Zoe was a breath of fresh air. That is what I love about this series the most, the characters and their real scenarios that are relative to life as we know it. Just an FYI, *GREED* serves as a bridge to the next four books in the series. You'll get to see Greene Gardens flourish from inception!

How was it getting to know Zoe a bit more? If you've read Loveless, the third continued story from my *Forbidden* series then you were briefly introduced to her. What I liked the most about Zoe was that she was so humble and giving. Always willing to be a source of light for others without expecting anything in return. It felt really good weaving in two different stories into *GREED*. Including the novel that honestly changed my life, *Last Comes Love,* was something I looked forward to doing the moment I knew Bryant would be a main character in *GREED*. *Last Comes Love* was such a hard story to write toward the end. I knew going into the novel, how it would end, but actually writing it took a toll on your girl during the writing process. And I know you felt it too. There was a funeral scene outlined and written for *Last Comes Love.* I decided to take the scene out of that novel because I believed it would be too much to handle in an already difficult story. You got to read that deleted funeral scene in *GREED*, but it was told from Zoe's perspective to make it less palpable.

I'm grateful to have been chosen to write the stories in this series. It took a couple of years of research but I'm very happy with the direction the books in this series is taking us. What did you think of *GREED*? Let me know with a review. I'm excited to read your thoughts!

If this is your first time reading a book by me, thank you for taking a chance and I hope you enjoyed yourself. If you did, you're what I like to call a Brookelynite, welcome! If you're a loyal reader who has been rocking with me from a book, two books, or many books ago, I am so grateful for your continued support. It's my soul food. Whether you're new or a loyal reader of mine, thank you so much for reading. I appreciate you. I write because I love it, but I also write for your love of reading. See you at the end of the next book.

Love,

Brookelyn.

About the Author

Brookelyn Mosley is a captivating voice in the world of black romance literature. With a gift for weaving heartfelt narratives and steamy encounters, she invites readers on journeys of love, passion, and self-discovery. Through her compelling storytelling, Brookelyn celebrates the beauty of black love and explores the complexities of relationships with authenticity and depth. With over 40+ titles, her stories resonate with true-blue readers, touching hearts and inspiring conversations about love, identity, and resilience.

Connect With Me Online!

Facebook: http://facebook.com/brookelynmosley
Facebook Reading Group: Brookelynites Book Lounge
Instagram: @Brookelynmosley
My Website: BrookelynMosley.com
My Readers Website: BKBookLounge.com
My Mailing List: BK Insiders